BRITTANY

BRITTANY
JACK WEYLAND

Deseret Book Company
Salt Lake City, Utah

Library of Congress Cataloging-in-Publication Data

Weyland, Jack, 1940–
    Brittany / by Jack Weyland.
        p.   cm.
    Summary: While trying to fit in at a new school and dreaming of college, being a Mormon missiony, and marriage, Brittany undergoes the trauma of date rape and its consequences.
    ISBN 1-57345-303X
    [1. Acquaintance rape—Fiction.   2. Rape—Fiction.   3. Dating violence—Fiction.   4. Interpersonal relations—Fiction.
    5. Mormons—Fiction.]   I. Title.
    PZ7.W538Br   1997
    [Fic]—dc21   97-30547
                                                                 CIP
                                                                 AC

Printed in the United States of America

10   9   8   7   6   5   4   3   2   1   49510

To the young woman
who lived Brittany's story
and to her mother, her counselor,
and her bishop

1

At seventeen, Brittany had hopes and dreams about what her life would be like. She hoped to do well enough in high school to get a scholarship to BYU, and then someday to perform with BYU's touring group, the Young Ambassadors. After graduating from BYU, she would serve a mission. Finally, she dreamed of marrying a returned missionary in the temple. She wanted her wedding night to be her first time, and his first time too. She and her husband would be happy together. They would be faithful, and they would raise a wonderful family.

She did not think her dreams were too much to hope for. She never wished for expensive clothes or flashy cars. Those things had never been that important to her.

The fulfillment of many of Brittany's dreams was still years away, but one that was very dear to her was about to come true.

The phone call came just after supper. "Brittany, this is Mr. Andrews. How are you doing tonight?"

"I'm fine." She could hardly stand the suspense.

"Good. Well, guess what?" Being a good drama coach, he paused to let the tension build.

He went on. "Brittany, I'm sure you've heard about Melissa's accident."

"Yes. I heard she broke her leg, skiing."

"That's right. It's going to be impossible for her to take her part in the play." He paused again. "I'm calling to see how you would feel about replacing her and taking on the role of Eliza Doolittle."

When Brittany got the word that Melissa had been hurt, she wondered what Mr. Andrews would do. Brittany had tried out for the part and felt good about her audition. Even though she was only a junior, Brittany had one advantage in the competition for the lead role in *My Fair Lady:* she resembled Audrey Hepburn, the actress who had played the role of Eliza Doolittle in the movie. Brittany had the same light complexion, the large expressive eyes, the long dark hair, and the slender, almost fragile physique of a young Audrey Hepburn. But Melissa was a senior, and Mr. Andrews had gone with the older girl.

"Brittany?"

"Yes, I'm here, Mr. Andrews. I guess I'm just a little stunned. I'd love to do it. Thank you."

"No need to thank me. You earned the chance. It's a demanding role, and you will have to work hard to catch up with the rest of the cast, but I have the utmost confidence in you. You have excellent stage presence, and, of course, a marvelous singing voice. I'm sure you'll be able to pull this off in grand style."

"I'll do my best, Mr. Andrews."

"I know you will. Oh, I've just finished talking to Craig. As you know, he's playing the part of Henry Higgins, and the two of you will have to do a lot of work together. You've lost two weeks already, so the quicker you can get up to speed, the better it will be for all of us. Can you meet with Craig before school for the next few days to go over your lines?"

"Yes. I can do that."

"Fine. I'll tell him. Is seven o'clock too early?"

"No, that'll be okay."

"You know Craig, don't you?" Mr. Andrews asked.

"A little bit. We're in choir together," she said. She wasn't sure what to make of Craig. He was obviously talented and very outgoing; in fact, that was the problem. He had *student leader* written all over him.

"I'll make arrangements with Craig for tomorrow. If you'd like, you can use my classroom. I'll phone the custodian and give him permission to let you in each morning. Well, again, congratulations. Work hard and do your best, and I'm sure we'll pull this thing together after all."

By the time Brittany showed up the next morning, Craig had already persuaded a custodian to open up Mr. Andrews's classroom. "Good morning," Craig said cheerfully. "You're right on time. Maybe we can just read through our lines today, if that's all right with you."

They sat down. Craig pulled out his planner and glanced at it.

A planner? Brittany thought. *Sure, that sounds about right for this guy.*

He had a long face and strong jaw. *I wonder if this is what Abraham Lincoln looked like in high school,* she thought. That impression was softened a little, though, by his sandy-colored hair, boyish grin, and blue eyes.

Craig put his planner away. "Well, I guess we'd better get started." He paused. "This is kind of awkward, isn't it?"

She smiled faintly. "Yes, it is, actually. Look, for whatever it's worth, I just want you to know I feel as bad as anyone about Melissa breaking her leg."

"Oh, I know that." He smiled. "It's not your fault." He stood up and began pacing the floor. Then, with a sudden theatrical flare, he turned and pointed at Britanny. "I mean it's not like you were hiding in the bushes on the ski slope, and jumped out and pushed her off the cliff just so you

3

could take over her part, right?" He leaned closer to confront her. "You didn't do that . . . or did you?"

Brittany pretended to break down. "Yes, yes, I did it! And I'm glad. She had it coming to her."

He turned to an imaginary off-stage and called out, "All right, Inspector, take her away. This case is solved."

Wow, Brittany thought. *This is the most fun I've had since we moved here.*

It was now February. Brittany had been attending Fairfield High School near Salt Lake City since September. She'd grown up in Grace, Idaho, but after her parents' divorce, she and her mother had moved because her mom couldn't find work there.

After Craig and Brittany had raced through the script for *My Fair Lady,* Craig said, "Eliza Doolittle is in almost every scene. Do you really think you can learn all this in time?"

"Sure, no problem," she said, trying her best to sound confident, even though she had some misgivings herself.

"You seem pretty sure of yourself."

"I know what I can do."

He smiled. "That's great. I like that in a person. That's the way I've always been." He set his script on the floor. "I probably shouldn't say anything, but some people don't think you should've gotten the part because you're only a junior and, also, because you're so new."

"I tried out for the part, just like everybody else. It seems fair to me."

"Good for you. You've got to have a winning attitude if you're going to succeed in life. That's one thing my dad has taught me."

"What does your dad do?" she asked.

"He's an attorney. How about your dad?"

Brittany usually didn't like to talk about her home life. "I don't know what my dad's doing now. He moved to Chicago after my mom and he got divorced."

Craig looked like he regretted bringing up the subject. "Sorry."

"It's no big deal. Not every family can be rich and happy."

"We're not rich."

"You ever notice how people with money always say that?" she asked. She tried to make it sound as though she was teasing, but, even so, there was a tinge of bitterness in her reply.

"I'm serious, we're not rich."

"You have your own car, though, right?" she asked.

"Yeah, but it's just an old clunker."

"And you don't have to work after school, do you?"

"No, but I work every summer."

"Where do you work?" she asked.

"I work for my dad."

"I mean a *real* job."

"It's a real job."

"And is Daddy training you so you can take over the business someday?"

Craig's grin vanished. "Is there anything wrong with that?"

"No, not really. But try wiping off tables and picking up garbage in the food court of a mall sometime. Then you'd know how easy you've got it."

He was about to object when the cellular phone in his backpack began ringing. It was his mother, reminding him of a dentist appointment he had later that morning.

Brittany had never known anyone her age with a cellular phone. "Nice phone," she teased after he hung up.

"Okay, fine, you win. My family *is* better off than yours. What do you want me to do about it, give you my car?"

She looked at him for a second, then said. "Hmmm . . . let me think about that. What year is your car?"

5

Craig had a good sense of humor, but he seldom laughed out loud. "Whoa! Good job."

"Mostly I joke around just with people I feel comfortable with," she said.

"So does that mean you're feeling a more at ease with me now that we've gotten to know each other a little better?" he asked.

"I guess so," she said, but then wondered if she was being honest. When he talked to her, he looked into her eyes and gave her his undivided attention. Very few boys she'd ever met did that. And yet it made her wonder if he'd learned it from some *You Too Can Succeed* video.

She appreciated his boyish grin and enjoyed looking into his blue eyes, and he certainly didn't seem to mind looking into hers. Even so, there was something else about him she didn't know how to deal with. He carried with him an aura of confidence. It was easy to believe that his parents had poured their best efforts and resources into him. He'd probably had every music lesson, summer camp, and educational field trip possible.

"Let me ask you a question," Craig asked. "How did you get here this morning?"

"My mom brought me."

Craig lightly struck his forehead with the palm of his hand. "Gosh, what a dummy I am. I should've made arrangements to pick you up. Sorry."

"It's okay. My mom has to be at work at seven anyway, so it worked out alright."

"Where does your mom work?"

"She's a manager at a dry cleaners."

"Which one?"

She looked away, trying to decide how to answer the question. Finally, she returned his gaze. "Why do you need to know that?"

"Just curious, that's all. Is that bad?"

"I was just imagining you promising to dirty a sweater and then drop it off at the cleaners, you know, just to help my mom and me out. I guess I don't want charity from you. We're doing all right."

"I hope you don't mind me saying this, but you really seem kind of defensive about all this."

She pursed her lips. "I guess I am. I've never been poor before. I don't know how I'm supposed to act."

Craig picked up his script from the floor and waved it in front of her. "Look, the whole point of *My Fair Lady* is that what really matters is what's inside you. Nothing else matters."

She was sitting with her arms folded, running her thumbnail across her front teeth. She did that whenever she was thinking about something. Her mother didn't approve and was always telling her to get her thumb out of her mouth. But it wasn't the thumb, just the thumbnail.

She looked up. Craig was still looking at her. "What are you thinking about?" he asked.

"Nothing."

"No, tell me. I really want to know."

She cocked her head and looked at him, not so much with suspicion, as surprise. "Why?"

"Because the better we know each other, the more effective we'll be on stage."

"And are you going to open yourself up to me?"

"Sure, if you want me to, I will, but I asked first. What were you thinking about just now?"

"Oh, I don't know, probably the same thing I'm always thinking about."

"And what's that?" he asked.

"That I wish I was back home—in Idaho."

"What town in Idaho?"

"Grace."

"You're kidding, right?"

She was puzzled. "What do you mean?"

"That means you've fallen from Grace."

"Gosh, Craig, that is so clever. Nobody has ever made a joke like that . . . only about every thirty seconds. For your information, Grace is not very far from Logan."

He couldn't let it go. "So, what's so amazing about Grace?" he teased.

She groaned but answered him, "It's small enough that you know everybody in town. Not like here."

"We're not so bad here, are we?"

"Have you ever moved?" she asked.

"No, I haven't. What's it like?"

"It's really hard sometimes. It's like it takes away your identity. Back home with my friends, I was a lot different than I am here."

"In what way?"

"I was more fun to be with. I mean like back home in school we kept thinking of things to do. They were mostly dumb, but at least it made it more fun."

"What kind of things?" he asked.

"One time we rolled a bowling ball down the hall. You can't believe how much noise that makes."

Craig, the ultimate listener, broke into a big smile. "A bowling ball? Are you serious? I'll have to try that sometime."

"And then on Fridays we'd all dress up to go to school. Like one Friday would be beach day, even though it might be in the middle of winter, or once we all came as irrigators, you know, wearing rubber boots." She smiled and shook her head. "It sounds dumb, but at least it made school fun."

"It sounds great, Brittany. It really does."

"It was." Her smile faded. "But here nobody knows me, and I feel like I have to fit in and be quiet and not say anything. Some days I can hardly make myself come to school. I don't know what I'd do if it weren't for choir and now this play."

"Let me help you."

"What can you do?"

He moved his chair closer. "I can introduce you to all my friends and get you more involved in things. You've got a lot of good ideas. I'm sure you could really make a difference here." He paused. "And from now on, for as long as we're coming early to practice, I'll pick you up. Okay?"

"Great."

"There's something you should know though." He looked embarrassed to even be saying it. "There's no reason for me to say this, but I think I'd better—just so we start off being honest with each other. I'm seeing someone now. Her name is Diana Briggs." He wiped his hand across his forehead. "That sounds so conceited, doesn't it? It's like me saying, *Look, I know you won't be able to help falling for me, so I'll tell you in advance, okay? There's no hope.*"

"Don't worry. I'll try to control myself, although I've got to tell you, it's driving me nearly out of my mind just being near you."

Craig's grin erupted into a laugh. "Really? What's the one thing about me that's driving you the most crazy?"

She'd noticed it earlier but hadn't said anything. "The fact that you're wearing one brown sock and one blue sock." She started giggling. "That's a nice touch, Craig."

He looked down at his feet, then slapped the side of his head. "Oh, no! I can't believe it! That's what I get for dressing in the dark."

"It'll be fine. When you're in class, just keep both feet on the floor and nobody'll notice."

A girl peeked through the window and then came into the room. "So this is where you two are hiding. You should've told me where you'd be, Craig. I've been looking all over for you."

This must be Diana, Brittany thought. *She must take after her father.*

It was not necessarily a compliment. Diana's features were strong—a dominant nose, dark, thick eyebrows, and full lips. For any given feature, Diana had more of it than Brittany—including a temper.

"Sorry," Craig said quickly.

Diana could not disguise her irritation at finding Craig and Brittany together. "I went down to the auditorium first, but it was locked, so then I didn't know where you two were hiding."

"We weren't hiding," Brittany said, not willing to buckle under Diana's anger. "Mr. Andrews gave us permission to be here. You could have asked the custodian. He knew where we were."

"Have you met Brittany yet?" Craig asked Diana.

"Not yet."

"Hi," Brittany said cautiously.

Diana started her inspection at eye level and then went slowly down and then back up. "I guess you probably know how bad all the seniors feel about Melissa breaking her leg. Some people are saying they won't go to the play just because Melissa isn't in it anymore."

"Oh, my gosh, Diana, why even bring that up?" Craig asked.

"No reason. I just thought she should know. Let's go, so we're not late," Diana said.

"You go, Diana. I'll catch up with you later."

"It's almost time for class," Diana grumbled. "I don't want to be late. And you shouldn't be either."

"Why don't you go to your locker and wait for me, and I'll be there in a minute."

"Fine then," Diana said, leaving in a huff, and slamming the door on her way out.

Craig was about to say something to Brittany, but, before he could, Mr. Andrews came in to get ready for his first period class, and they left.

While walking Brittany to her locker, Craig said, "I'm sorry about Diana. She gets that way sometimes."

"No problem."

"Look, I'll pick you up tomorrow morning, okay?" he asked.

"Sure. Thanks for your help."

"About ten to seven?" he asked.

After a pause, Brittany said, "I don't want to cause any trouble between you and Diana."

"It'll be fine. Don't worry about it."

"Okay, thanks. It will make it easier for my mom if you pick me up."

As soon as they got to her locker, he said good-bye, took two steps, and then turned around to ask, "You can't see my socks when I'm standing, can you?"

She cocked her head to the side and looked at his feet. "No, not at all."

"Maybe I'll just stand in the back of all my classes today."

She grinned. "Good idea, Craig. I'm sure nobody would notice that."

The next morning Craig picked her up. Once they got to the classroom he brought out some cinnamon buns his mom had made the night before, and a carton of orange juice and two paper cups.

"You didn't need to go to so much trouble," Brittany said.

"No problem," he said. "Actually, it was my mom's idea. Besides, I need you healthy for the play."

Craig pulled up his pant legs. "Look, matching socks. Pretty good, huh? Not only that, but I got dressed all by myself. Impressive, right?"

"Absolutely. Gosh, your mom and dad must be so proud of you. I bet before long your dad will even take the training wheels off your bike."

He shook his head. "No, no, it's too soon. I'm not ready for that yet."

"Sure, I understand. You have to take things a little at a time."

Once they finished eating, Craig picked up his script. "You want to get to work now?"

They finished a little early that day because Craig needed to study. While he worked at a desk, Brittany wandered around the room. Out of boredom, she turned on the overhead projector, pulled down the screen, and began making a shadow-bunny silhouette on the wall with her hand. Speaking in a high squeaky voice, she said, "Hi there, Craig. I'm a little bunny, and I've come to visit you."

He looked up. "I've got a test today."

Again in her high voice, she said, "Bunnies never have tests."

"What do bunnies do?"

"Bunnies hop." She made her shadow-bunny hop around the screen. "Hop, hop, hop."

Craig smiled and shut his book. "I'm going to flunk out because of you. You know that, don't you?"

Still in her high voice, she said, "Be like me. Bunnies never flunk. Come and play with me in Shadow-Land, and we'll hop around and smell the flowers and have fun all day long. Hop, hop, hop."

Craig spoke in a high sing-song voice. "Little bunny, what do I have to do to be with you in Shadow-Land?"

"Just make a little shadow animal with your hands, that's all."

"Okay. How about this?" He made a blob with his fist and mimicked the hopping motion of her shadow-bunny.

"What kind of shadow animal are you?" she asked in her bunny voice.

"I'm a little shadow-puppy," he said in his high voice.

"You don't look like a shadow-puppy," she said.

"What do I look like?"

"Actually . . . if you want the truth, you look like a fist."

In his deepest voice, Craig said, "I am a fist! In fact, I'm Fist Monster! I go around bopping little shadow-bunnies who make fun of my shape."

Brittany could hardly get the words out. "So—you bop—and I hop, right?"

"That's right, little shadow-bunny. And your time to be bopped has come!" He made a sudden move and grabbed her hand. "Bop, bop, bop."

"Help me! help me!" she squealed in a high voice.

"There, maybe that will teach you a lesson," he said, letting her go.

"Mister Fist Monster, would you like me to show you how to be a cute little shadow-puppy?"

"Sure, why not?"

She arranged his hand into something which, on the screen, resembled a dog.

"We're a little bunny and a little puppy, and all the day long, we hop through the daffodils and the roses," she said, sounding again like Minny Mouse.

"What do we eat when we get hungry?" Craig asked in his high voice.

Brittany placed a breath mint on top of the overhead projector. It made an image on the screen. "We eat little shadow-candies." She moved the mouth of her shadow-bunny over the mint. "Ummh, good, yum, yum."

Craig grabbed the mint from the projector and put it in his very real mouth.

She returned to her natural voice. "I can't believe this—you would take food from a defenseless little shadow-bunny? That is so pathetic."

Craig smiled. "That's right. Got any more?"

"Little shadow-bunny is not happy with you," she said in her high voice.

"Oh man, this is so weird," Craig said in his normal voice. "If anyone sees us, they're going to put us away. And then what will we do?"

"Knowing us, we'll put on a musical for the other patients."

Craig stared at her for a moment, then said, "You're so much fun,"

"Thank you." She answered in her high bunny voice but then dropped down to her regular voice. "Excuse me. Thank you."

"Diana and I never do fun things like this."

"Does she have a planner too?"

"Afraid so."

"Somehow I knew she would," Brittany said. "I know this was dumb, but it was fun for me. I haven't done anything like this since we moved here. Back home, with my friends, we used to do things like this all the time. I guess maybe I'm feeling more comfortable now—at least with you anyway. So that's good."

"You're friends with Megan and Andrea, though, aren't you? I know you eat lunch with 'em."

She didn't know if she should talk about it or not. "Yeah, we're friends, but it's not the same."

"How come?"

"I don't know. I just can't talk to them like I could with my friends back home."

"Can you talk to me?"

"Yeah, I can, pretty much."

"Let me be your friend then," he said. They were gazing into each other's eyes. Brittany felt like she should break eye contact but for some reason she couldn't turn away. Or, more truthfully, she didn't want to.

Finally Shadow-bunny hopped away, only to be intercepted again by the Fist Monster. And that's where things stood when Diana looked in the room. She saw Craig and

Brittany standing in front of the screen, holding hands and looking into each other's eyes.

She yanked the door open and barged in. "So, what are you two working on today? Funny, I don't remember this part in the script."

With his face turning bright red, Craig, turned off the projector. "We finished a little early. Brittany was showing me how to make a shadow-animal."

Diana's words poured out in an angry stream. "Brittany, you're such a talented girl. And you're so full of surprises, aren't you? Today I come and you and Craig are holding hands. I can't wait to see what you'll be doing with him tomorrow."

Brittany tried to salvage the situation. "We really weren't holding hands. What happened was Craig was Fist Monster and I was Shadow-bunny, and . . . "

Diana shook her head. "Look, I really don't have time for this, okay? C'mon, Craig, let's go. Maybe this practicing before school isn't such a good idea. If Brittany wants to learn her part, maybe she should work on it at home, like everybody else."

That afternoon at practice Craig was more reserved around Brittany. He asked if it would be all right if they didn't meet anymore before school. Brittany said that would be fine.

She didn't blame Craig. The way Diana was, it would be hard to turn her down for anything.

Diana the Avenger, she thought with a smile. *I wonder if she has any Viking blood in her?*

The next two weeks passed like a blur for Brittany. The play was taking up all her time and energy. Though she and Craig spent a lot of time together in rehearsals, they were both very much aware of Diana and how much she resented Brittany. They tried hard to stay detached, but it wasn't easy.

There's something about being in a play that brings people together.

The script called for Henry Higgins and Eliza Doolittle to fall in love, but not to show it openly. The play was almost too much like real life. Because of Diana, whatever feelings were generated between Craig and Brittany had to be disguised. It was clear that Diana had friends in the cast who reported back everything that happened at practices.

Brittany wondered how Craig really felt about her. He pretty much ignored her around school, but when they were onstage together, there was a great deal of romantic tension between them. Even the members of the stage crew, who did their best to ignore the play, quit talking to watch the fireworks when Craig and Brittany got together.

On the night of their dress rehearsal, about ten minutes before they were to begin, Brittany was standing in the wings, nervously going over her lines. Craig approached her.

"Did you get the changes Mr. Andrews wanted us to make tonight?" he asked.

By now Brittany recognized the deadpan look Craig got on his face when he was trying to pull something.

"Gosh, no, Craig. Tell me," she said, keeping a straight face.

"Well, in the last scene, instead of me asking you to bring my slippers, Mr. Andrews wants me to ask you to marry me."

"And what do I do? Laugh in your face?"

"No, of course not. You fall into my arms and tell me how grateful you are to me for giving meaning to your life, and then, with tears in your eyes, you tell me that from now on you'll dedicate every waking hour to my happiness."

She burst out laughing. "What's the matter, Craig, have a tough day? Haven't enough people told you how wonderful you are?"

"I'm totally serious." he persisted. "Mr. Andrews wants

the play to end with us in each other's arms, kissing." He cleared his throat. "Actually, and I'm not making this up, he suggested we practice kissing on our own time, so we get it right."

She placed her hand on his chest and, with a smile, pushed him away. "That is so cheesy, Craig."

Craig looked hurt. "You doubt me? Look, if you don't believe me, just ask Mr. Andrews."

"Actually, I just saw him, and he didn't say anything about this," she said.

"Well, he's got a lot on his mind right now. He asked me to tell you. I think we should start practicing right away."

"Really? And what would Diana think about that?" Brittany asked.

Craig's smile faded. "She knows that what we do on stage is just acting."

"So, even if we kissed on stage, that would be okay with her, right?"

"Sure, no problem."

"And what about you? Could you kiss me and just think of it in strictly professional terms?"

Craig gave her his best noble and sincere look. "Well, as you know, acting is my life."

"Yeah, right."

"Look, if you don't believe me about the changes, we can go and ask Mr. Andrews, okay?"

She knew he was bluffing. "All right, let's do that."

Craig glanced at the backstage clock. "It's too late now. We're almost ready to begin. So what do you say? When do you want to get together and practice?"

"Some parts are very demanding. You know, like playing a psycho killer or doing a kissing scene with you—both would be equally tough."

"Gosh, thanks a lot."

"You deserve it, Craig, and you know it."

17

"I can't believe how mean you are to me," he said. "You should respect me."

"Why's that?"

"I'm your leader."

Brittany shook her head. "I don't think so."

"How can you say that? Do I need to remind you that I'm senior class president?"

She gave him her best dramatic sigh. "Actually, you tell me that about every ten minutes. It's sad, really, how some people *need* to be president of something, just to prop up their pitifully low self-esteem."

"But wait, that's not all! I'm also a member of the student senate."

"Really? Well, I didn't vote for you." It was, of course, true. The election had been held the previous spring, before Brittany had moved down from Idaho.

"You didn't? I'm crushed," Craig said.

"You'll get over it."

"Can I be serious for a moment?" he asked.

"Gosh, I don't know, can you?"

He reached for her hand.

"Oh, no, it's Fist Monster!" she cried out in her high voice.

He started laughing. "C'mon, Brittany, I really do want to be serious now. Okay?"

She cleared her throat ceremoniously. "Yes, of course. We will now be serious . . . very serious . . . extremely serious . . . deadly serious . . . "

"Well, maybe not *that* serious." He looked into her eyes. "I just want you to know how great it's been working with you."

Brittany felt a sudden rush of emotion. She took a deep breath, then said, "Thanks, it's been fun for me too." She didn't dare say more. It was no use talking about how much she liked him. The only reason they were together was because of the play. And when that was over, he would, most likely, go back to Diana.

"You're right about one thing, Craig. The way the play ends now isn't very satisfying," she said.

"How do you think it should end?" he asked.

"How about if I get rich and hire you to be my gardener?" Brittany teased.

"Your gardener?"

"Yeah, that seems fair." She spoke as the refined Eliza Doolittle. "Henry, have you weeded the tomahtos yet?" She pronounced tomato with an upper-crust British accent.

"That'd never work. I like it better the way it is now where I ask you to bring my slippers and you instantly obey."

She laughed. "Dream on."

"It could happen. You're kind of young now, but I'm sure that after you gain a little more wisdom, you'll come to appreciate me."

She wanted to slam him with a great comeback, but she noticed that, although he had the same teasing smile on his face she'd seen so many times, this time his eyes were serious. "Maybe so," she said quietly.

Because of Diana, she knew there was nothing more either of them could say, but it didn't stop them from gazing into each other's eyes. Before, when he'd looked at her that way, she'd always turned away, but this time she didn't. She met his gaze.

"I love your face," he said quietly. "And I love to hear you sing."

"I really enjoy singing with you."

"You're so beautiful."

She looked away. "Not really."

"You are."

She put her thumbnail to her teeth to give her some time to think, but then, remembering that her mom thought it looked dumb, she dropped her hand. No boy had ever told her she was beautiful before. Of course, the boys she knew in Idaho didn't say things like that. She didn't really know how to respond but finally came up with, "Well, thanks . . . I guess."

"You have so much to offer, so many talents. You need to come help us in student government. You'd really be great."

"So you're recruiting me for committee work, right? Is *that* what this is all about?"

Craig threw his hands in the air. "Oh, man, I never say the right thing."

She enjoyed watching Craig struggle to find something to say. She knew that seldom happened.

"Just say it, Craig."

He put out both his hands in front of him, palms up. It was an invitation that she accepted. She placed her hands on his. Neither one of them said anything as they stood holding hands and looking into each other's eyes.

Seconds passed. Someone brushed past them. A trumpet player in the pit orchestra kept going over a hard part again and again. Brittany looked around and saw a girl glaring at her. *She must be Diana's spy,* she thought.

Just then, Mr. Andrews, stormed into the back stage area. "People, let's get started! We don't want to be here all night. C'mon! C'mon! Act one—scene one. Everybody get to their places. I'm going into the audience to watch. You've got three minutes."

The dress rehearsal went badly. In the first act nearly a minute went by while Craig and Brittany were standing onstage, trading their lines in near total darkness. Cues were missed, and a piece of scenery even fell down.

After the rehearsal, Craig drove Brittany home. They were more reserved around each other and rode in silence.

Brittany knew it was because of Diana. She decided to face the issue. "What night is Diana coming?" she asked.

"Tomorrow and Saturday."

"My mom is coming tomorrow night. She'd come all three nights if she could, but she works at the temple on Fridays. I'm pretty sure she'll come to the Saturday night performance too."

"Do you know how good you are onstage?" he asked.

"Not really."

"I swear, you could carry the play if the entire cast were replaced by chimpanzees."

"Yeah, but if we used chimpanzees in the cast, who would be left to run the lights?"

A smile broke across his face. "I'm really going to miss talking to you."

"Me too."

"Maybe I shouldn't be saying this, but sometimes when we're doing a scene together, I wish it could last forever. One time I found myself pretending I really was Henry Higgins and you were Eliza, and we were doing a play about two high school students who live in Utah." He cleared his throat. "That's really dumb, isn't it?"

"No, not really."

"I wouldn't mind if there was some kind of time warp and we could end up as Henry and Eliza together. Would you?"

"No, but I wouldn't let you talk down to me, like you do in the play."

"I'd change for you," he said.

"You don't have to be in a play to change, you know."

"I know. I've been thinking about it."

"About what?"

"I've been thinking about maybe telling Diana I want to spend some time with other girls."

"Why would you do that?"

21

"Because all I can think about anymore is you," he said.

"Look, let's be real careful, okay. This happens all the time to actors. Two weeks from now any feelings we have for each other will have mostly disappeared."

"You really think so?"

She thought about admitting how much she liked him, but decided against it. She really did believe things would cool down between them after the play was over. It was tempting to ride this wave to the end, but she decided to be realistic. "Oh, sure, in a few days. You'll see."

They pulled up in front of where Brittany and her mother lived. It was a small rental house in a neighborhood that was beginning to get a bad reputation. It wasn't much, but it was all they could afford for now. Brittany was always embarrassed to have Craig see the place.

He walked her to the door. She wondered if he'd kiss her. In one way she hoped he would. But then she thought about seeing him in two or three weeks, walking down the hall, holding hands with Diana. He'd see her and look away, embarrassed to remember. She didn't want that to happen. If nothing else, she wanted to stay friends with him. She didn't think that would happen if every time he saw her, he remembered kissing her and felt guilty for betraying Diana.

She wanted him to understand how she felt. "Craig, I don't think that right now we can tell the difference between what's reality and what's happening just because we're in a play together. Let's not do anything we'll be embarrassed about after the play is over. Okay?"

"Yeah, sure, whatever you say. I'll respect your wishes."

"Thanks." She had her hand on the door and was about to go inside.

"I would like to talk to you though," he said. "About something else if that's okay."

She let go of the door. "All right."

"It might be warmer in the car," he said.

They returned to the car. He started the engine and ran the heater. "Here's the deal. Diana isn't that excited about me going on a mission. She thinks we ought to get married a few months after high school. She has some money coming from a family trust. She gets it this summer. We could get married, both go to college, and not have to work or anything. She says she doesn't want to lose me."

"What do *you* want to do?" Brittany asked.

Craig didn't answer immediately. He stared vacantly at the steering wheel and then turned to face her. "I really want to go on a mission."

"That's what you should do then."

"I know, but, the thing is, Diana and I have been seeing each other since we were in ninth grade. And it's been good, but right now, it'd be better for me to have someone like you, who really wanted me to go on a mission, and would encourage and support me." He paused. "If I really want to go on a mission, then I'm thinking it'd be better for me to break up with her. What I need now is a friend."

"But how can you just walk away from her? She must really care about you."

"Yeah, I guess she does."

"And you care about her, right?"

"Yeah, I guess."

"Then explain to me again how you came to the conclusion that you need to break up with her."

"Because she doesn't want me to go on a mission."

"I think you've got to talk to her then and tell her how you feel."

"What would I say?" he asked.

"Well, that's up to you, but you could say, Diana, I've decided to go on a mission. Will you support me in that decision?"

"She'll try to talk me out of it."

"You can always tell her you've made up your mind. I

don't think you should just dump her without trying to work something out. She loves you, Craig. Anybody can see that."

"I thought you'd encourage me to go ahead and break up with her."

"I want us to be friends, even if you are going with Diana. And the only way that can happen is if I tell you what I think is best."

They walked to the front door again. "You are a good friend," he said on the doorstep. They hugged each other and then he opened the door for her to go in.

Brittany was in a great mood. She grabbed an apple from the fridge on the way through the kitchen and then went to the door of her mother's bedroom. Her mother usually went to bed early because she had to be to work so early every morning. She might have been asleep but didn't admit to it when Brittany opened the door and quietly called out, "Mom, are you awake? I'm home."

Her mother sat up in bed and turned on the light. "How did it go tonight?"

"Okay I guess. It was a little rough, but I think it's going to be really good."

"I'm sure it will."

"Did you phone Dad and ask him if he could come?" Brittany asked.

"Yes, I did." A long pause. "He told me to tell you that this isn't a good time of year for him to get away."

Brittany wasn't surprised. "Sure, I understand."

"But he sends his love and wishes you the very best."

"Sure he does. It's fine, either way." She paused. "Craig and I had a good talk tonight."

"How do you feel about him?"

"We're friends. I hope we can become better friends before he leaves on his mission."

"I'm glad you have a friend like him."

"Thanks, Mom. Good night."

Brittany got ready for bed. She thumbed through a magazine while she ate her apple and then had a snack of graham crackers and milk. It was something she'd liked from the time she was a little girl. It reminded her of their home in Idaho. Their house was located five miles out of town in a canyon, a beautiful place in any season, especially so in the winter, with the snow sitting in heavy clumps on the branches of the big pine tree near their house.

Brittany washed her face and brushed her teeth and then returned to her room. She set her alarm, then got down on her knees by her bed to say her prayers.

Brittany loved Heavenly Father. She felt he was always there for her, especially when she had problems. She'd felt the Spirit many times in her life—in seminary class, when she read the scriptures in her room before going to bed, and whenever she knelt in prayer at the beginning or end of each day. She knew beyond any doubt that Heavenly Father loved her and cared about what happened to her. She knew he was listening to her as she poured out her heart to him and asked him for help. She had felt his love. It was not something she talked about, but it was there, and it was real. He'd answered her prayers before, and she knew he'd do it again as she asked him to help her do a good job in the play.

I can do anything with Heavenly Father's help, she thought as she finished her prayer and crawled into bed, underneath a quilt her grandmother had made for her, decorated with an embossed image of the Idaho Falls temple and the words *The House of the Lord.* Gradually, her bed warmed up, and Brittany felt herself drifting off.

All I have to do is think positive and trust in Heavenly Father, she thought, just before falling asleep.

2

The next day, Thursday, was clear, bright and cold. To get the other students excited about attending the play, members of the cast came to school dressed in what they would be wearing onstage. Because Brittany would go from rags to riches, she had a choice of costumes. She decided to go as the girl who sold flowers in the marketplace in the first scene.

She saw a couple leaning against the wall by her locker. The guy had his arm around the girl. "Excuse me, Gov'nuh, but could I interest you in a flower for your laidy friend?"

He seemed annoyed at being disturbed. "Not really."

"What's the matter, Gov'nuh? You bought one for the other girl I seen you with yesterday."

The girl was enjoying this. "He was with another girl?" she asked.

"Oh, yes, ma'am. He goes through 'em like fish 'n chips, this one does. He's quite the laidy's man, if you ask me." As Brittany walked away, she dropped her Cockney accent. "Just kidding. You guys be sure and come to the play tonight, okay?"

In biology class Brittany sat in the middle of the row nearest the door. On the first day of the class, when she hadn't known anyone, she was grateful when the boy in front of her had turned around to speak.

"Hi, I'm Derek. How come we haven't met?" he asked.

"I'm Brittany," she said. She meant to add that she was new in school and had just moved in. It came out, "I'm *smew* in school." She grimaced, put her hand over her mouth, then started to laugh.

"Come again?" he said.

"I guess I'm a little nervous."

"Hey, not to worry. We're all friendly folks here." He grinned, and she noticed that he looked a little like the actor who starred in the TV show *Highlander*. Derek was tall, muscular, had a rugged face, and wore his black hair long.

From then on, Derek always spoke to her in class. He was friendly at a time when she needed a friend, and she appreciated him being nice to her. But there was also something about him that kind of bugged her. Derek talked mostly about himself, in a bragging sort of way. He told her he was in a rock band, but when she asked around, nobody else in school had ever heard of the group.

"So what's with the outfit?" he asked when she sat down the day the play opened.

"I'm in the play tonight, that's all."

"No kidding? Are you like the star of the show?" he asked.

She paused. She didn't want to sound conceited. "Well, yeah, I guess you could say that."

"Looks like I'll have to go then, don't it?"

"You don't have to, but it'd be great if you did. Who knows? You might even like it."

"I'm not much for things like that. What kind of play is it?"

"It's a musical."

He made a pained expression. "You mean like an opera?"

"No, we talk and sing. In an opera, they just sing."

He crumpled a piece of paper into a tiny ball. "Is it really boring?"

"Not really. At least I don't think it is."

"I might go, just to see you," he said, as he gently lobbed the ball of paper in her direction.

She dodged the paper ball. "It's tonight, Friday, and Saturday."

"I'll make a deal with you. If I go to this play of yours, then you have to go out with me sometime. Okay?"

"Gosh, I don't know, Derek." She couldn't help laughing. "They did ask us to try to get people to come to the play, but I'm not sure they wanted me to make that much of a sacrifice, just to fill one more seat."

"Oh, come on, we'll just go to a movie with some friends, that's all. It's no big deal."

Brittany tried to decide what to tell him. After Saturday, when the play would be over, she wouldn't have much to look forward to. She was resigned to the fact that Craig and Diana would stay together. So maybe it wouldn't be so bad to go to a movie with Derek. She hadn't had an official date since she moved from Idaho. And only two or three dates there.

Derek was taller than Craig and probably outweighed him by fifty pounds. He had big hands that often had either dirt or engine grease under the fingernails. His hair was longer than most boys in school. Brittany wouldn't have minded that, but he didn't take good care of it. She kept wanting to suggest he use a conditioner, but she didn't know how he'd take it.

Derek wasn't her ideal guy, but he wasn't that bad either. For one thing, he had great cheek bones that gave a certain dramatic quality to his face. Also, he talked to her every day. That was more than most people did.

She wasn't sure what his standards were, but she wasn't afraid to ask.

"I might agree to it, Derek, but I should tell you, I don't go to R-rated movies."

He looked hurt. "And you think I do?"

"Not really. I just wanted you to know, that's all."

"Look, you can even pick the movie. How about it? We could double with one of my friends."

"You know Craig Weston, don't you?" she asked.

"Yeah, sure."

"He's in the play too. Maybe we could double with him and Diana."

"No problem. Craig and me are buddies."

It encouraged her to know that Derek and Craig were friends. "Well, okay, you got yourself a deal."

Almost immediately after agreeing to go out with Derek, she had misgivings. He had kind of a rough side to him that she didn't appreciate. Like the first day of class. Derek had tapped a boy next to him on the shoulder and showed him a nude figure of a woman in the textbook. He said, "I think I'm going to like this class. How about you?"

That is so juvenile, Brittany had thought at the time.

During the last half of class they had a quiz. Brittany didn't know any of the answers because she'd been so busy with rehearsals, she hadn't done any homework all week. She told that to Derek when the teacher announced a quiz.

"Don't worry about it. I take care of my friends."

She did her best on the quiz, but after answering one of the questions, she realized she didn't know any of the other answers. She turned her paper over, looked up, and saw that Derek had written big and was leaning to the side so she could see his paper. He was making it easy for her to copy his answers.

Brittany wasn't tempted, not only because it went against everything she'd been taught, but also because the teacher gave these kind of quizzes once or twice a week. He also threw their two worst scores away. Brittany had done well on the others, so it really wouldn't hurt her grade to flunk one. Besides, she had a good excuse.

As she got up to leave after class, Derek quietly asked, "Did you get it all?"

"No. Thanks anyway though."

"I was just trying to help out, that's all."

"I know. Thanks, but I've never been very good at cheating."

"I know, me either. See you tonight at the play."

Her next class was choir. Mr. Garcia excused those who were in the play. He didn't want them using their singing voices since they'd be singing so much that night.

Megan, Andrea, and Brittany decided to go to early lunch in the school cafeteria. It would give them an hour and a half to sit around and talk.

Andrea had a round face, was always wishing she were taller, sang alto in the choir, got straight A's in school, wore expensive clothes, and criticized those who didn't. Megan, on the other hand, was much smaller, had short, light brown hair, and sang soprano in choir. In many ways, Megan looked like she needed one more growth spurt to finally push her into full-blown adolescence.

Brittany felt as though Andrea and Megan were becoming her friends, but it still wasn't like her friends back in Idaho. Andrea came from a good family and was active in the Church. She did everything she was supposed to, but one thing that bothered Brittany was how critical she was of other people. Sometimes when they were eating lunch, Andrea would see someone and say sarcastically, "Nice outfit." She would then point out some girl. Brittany knew what she was supposed to say—how bad the girl looked. Usually Megan played the game, but Brittany never did.

While they were eating, Andrea said to Brittany, "Oh, I drove by your house last night."

Brittany knew what Andrea meant. The house was small and wasn't in the best part of town.

"We're just living there until our house is finished," Brittany said. She realized it was the first time she'd lied to impress someone since she was a little girl.

"Oh, you're having a house built? I didn't realize that," Andrea said. "Where?"

Brittany named a place over by the mall where she'd seen new homes being built. That seemed to satisfy Andrea.

"Did you hear about Kristin?" Andrea asked.

"No, what?" Megan said.

"She's pregnant. Can you believe that?"

"Who's the father?" Brittany asked.

"Who do you think?"

Brittany shook her head in frustration at the mind games Andrea was playing all the time. "I have no idea."

"Matt. They started going together last summer. I'm not surprised. Not surprised at all. I saw her and Matt once at a party. They were totally out of control. I mean *totally*."

"She must feel really bad. Have you talked to her?" Brittany asked.

Andrea seemed insulted. "Why would I do that?"

"I don't know. Maybe just to give her some support."

Andrea scoffed. "I'm not a social worker, okay? Besides, what would I tell her? *Too bad you messed up?*"

Brittany didn't know what made her feel worse, that Kristin had compromised her standards, or that Andrea took such delight in it.

Brittany wasn't exactly sure why Andrea treated her as a friend. It wasn't like Andrea to seek out new people at school and make friends with them. The only reason Brittany could think of was because she was now recognized as one of the best singers in choir. *Maybe that's the reason,* she thought.

There are a lot of people out there. I hope I don't mess up, Brittany thought as she stood off-stage, waiting for the performance to begin. The school auditorium was so full, people were standing in the back.

Brittany was excited and nervous at the same time. Her hands were clammy and her heart was beating fast. She felt like she might get sick, but this happened every time just before she performed, so she was almost used to it. Besides, this was what she had always dreamed of. Ever since the time when she was in third grade and her mother had taken her to a high school play, she had wanted to star in a musical play. She had fantasized about being the girl who sang all the solos and fell in love, and, in spite of overwhelming odds, ended up marrying the hero. And now her dream was about to become reality.

She moved the curtain and peeked into the audience trying to find her mother. In the process she saw Derek. He was there with some of his friends. He was laying back in his seat with his legs sprawled into the aisle. It made him appear disrespectful, and she didn't like the looks of the boys he was with.

Because Derek had come to the play, she knew he'd insist she go out with him. She didn't look forward to being with him, but told herself, *It's only one time, and, with any luck, we'll be doubling with Craig and Diana.*

Finally, she located her mother in the audience. She had come by herself but was sitting in a section with several other parents and was chatting with a woman next to her. Brittany wondered if any of the people she was sitting with would recognize her as the woman they took their dirty clothes to. Brittany's family had been much better off in

Idaho, before the divorce. Not rich, but better off than they were now. It was hard not to have any extra money.

Andrea and Megan were also in the play, but they didn't have any speaking parts. They were part of the chorus in the big scenes. Megan came up to her and gave her a hug. With her arms still around her, she said, "Good luck. Not that you need luck. I know you'll do a great job."

"Thanks."

Andrea saw Megan and Brittany standing together. She didn't like to be left out of anything. She came over right away. "What's going on?" she asked.

"I was just wishing Brittany good luck," Megan said.

Andrea nodded. "Right. Me too. Here, let me fix this." She took a tissue from a shirt pocket and rubbed it on a spot on Brittany's cheek. "You had a little blob of makeup on your face. There, I got it off."

"Thanks. Anything else?"

"Turn around. Let me check you out."

Brittany turned around.

"I'm not wild about what they picked for you to wear, but I guess it'll have to do."

"I'm supposed to look down on me luck," Brittany said, using the accent she had practiced for the play.

"She looks fine," Megan said.

"If you say so, Megan," Andrea said sarcastically. "I should've tried out for your part," Andrea said to Brittany.

Standing behind Andrea, Megan rolled her eyes.

Brittany was tempted to say something cutting, but she didn't. "You should've, Andrea. You'd have been really good."

"Oh, well, too late now. I need to talk to someone else. See you later."

They watched her go.

"There wasn't anything on your face," Megan said. "I

don't know why she does that. Also, does she honestly think she can sing as good as you can?"

"I guess so."

"Not even her daddy can buy her a singing voice."

"Does she ever talk about me when I'm not around?" Brittany asked.

"How do you mean?"

"Does she ever criticize me?"

Megan hesitated. "Sometimes."

"I thought she probably did."

"She's just jealous. You're too much competition for her. You know that, don't you? You're cuter, more talented, and nicer to people than she'll ever be. You're going to be so good tonight. I'm serious."

Brittany gave Megan a hug. "Thanks. I needed that."

Megan left, and Brittany looked around for Craig. He was standing off in a corner by himself. She walked over to him, put her hand on his arm, and asked, "How you doin'?"

"Okay, I guess. I'm a little nervous though."

"It'll be alright once we get started."

He nodded.

She leaned into him and chucked him lightly under the chin with her fist. "It's going to be okay. The important thing is to have fun. If you want, I know a game we can play tonight. It's called 'Magic Word.' We agree on a word that's not in the script, and we each try to say that word during the play. The one who says it the most times, wins."

"What's the word?" he asked.

"You decide. It can be anything, just whatever we decide."

Craig smiled. "I've got one. The word is *auto*."

"Auto?"

"Yes, but remember the play takes place before cars were invented, so it's not going to be easy."

"Auto it is then," she said.

"I'm going to win," he said.

"Not a chance."

"Why do you say that?" he asked.

"It's my game."

A few minutes later it was time to begin. The house lights dimmed and the orchestra began playing the overture. In a few seconds, Eliza Doolittle, poor but plucky, would walk onto the stage and try to sell some flowers.

Brittany peeked once more out into the auditorium. With the house lights out and a spotlight shining in her eyes, she couldn't even see the audience.

She took a deep breath. For a brief instant, Brittany wondered what life would be like if she hadn't moved. Her school would have had a musical too, and she would have been in it. The only difference would be that everyone in the small high school would have been in the musical, and, second, the people there were really her friends. She'd known them since she was little. They'd grown up together. The friends she had now were friends just because of choir and the play.

But life must go on. She wasn't in Idaho anymore. She was here, and in a musical. She was one of the stars, and this was her cue to enter the stage and become Eliza Doolittle.

She entered, stage right.

The "Magic Word" game helped Craig and Brittany get over their first-night jitters. Brittany scored early in the first act when she was supposed to say, "He ought to be ashamed of himself . . . " She winked privately at Craig and said, "He *auto* be ashamed of himself . . . "

Craig grimaced but went on with his lines. A few minutes later he changed the words of his song from, "She should be taken out and hung for the cold-blooded murder of the English tongue!" to, "She *auto* be taken out and hung . . . "

No one seemed to notice what they were doing, but during the few times they were offstage together, they enjoyed a laugh while each claimed to be ahead in the game.

Somewhere in the second act, Brittany thought, *This is so great!* She hadn't counted on how much energy the audience would give her. They were very appreciative of the songs she sang and the dialogue where she used the thick Cockney accent she had been working on for so long. They loved the romantic tension between her and Craig. At times it seemed like something you could almost reach out and touch.

The cast members were all very supportive of each other. When someone came off stage, others in the cast let them know what a good job they'd done. And that was true of everyone, not just the main parts. Everyone was working together to make this as good as possible. They were having fun.

Brittany's only regret was that she would only get to do the play two more times, and then it would be over. She didn't know what she was going to do to fill her time. Of course, she did know. She'd go back to working regular hours at the mall, start doing homework again, and begin helping more around the house. But none of that would be as exciting as this.

When the last line was spoken, and the curtain closed, the audience gave them a standing ovation. Of course they were the mothers, fathers, and classmates of the cast, but still, it was a standing ovation.

Finally, the applause ended. Some friends and family came behind the curtains to congratulate the performers. Brittany's mother came backstage and hugged her and told her again and again what a wonderful job she'd done. Diana, along with her folks, came to congratulate him.

Brittany was about to go to the dressing room when

Derek sauntered up to her. He smiled and said, "Good job, Brittany. I really enjoyed watching you prance around onstage."

Brittany thought it was a strange thing to say. She would have expected him to say something about her voice or compliment her on her acting.

"I brought you something," he said, awkwardly thrusting a rose into her hand.

"Thanks, Derek. That's real thoughtful of you."

"No problem," he said. "I know girls like flowers."

"Thanks," she said.

"Well," he said, "I did my part of our agreement, so you got to do yours. When do you want to go out with me?" he asked.

"We're going to double with Craig and Diana, right? That's what you said when we made the agreement."

"No problem. How about next Saturday night? We could go to the movie or something, and then maybe go back to my place for something to eat."

"Okay, I'll talk to you on Monday."

"Could you wear something from the play?" he asked.

Brittany was curious. "Why? What would you like to have me wear?"

"What you wore right there at first, on the street, when you were selling flowers in the market."

"Not the gown I wore at the ball later in the play?" Brittany asked.

"No, the rag costume. I liked that the best. And I liked the way you talked, right there at the beginning. That was real good."

"Sorry, we have to send everything back to the place we rented it all from."

"Bummer. So, what movie do you want to see?" he asked.

"I don't even know what's playing, but I usually like Disney movies."

"That's what we'll see then."

A few minutes later Brittany was taking off her makeup in the dressing room. Andrea made a big show of coming in and throwing her arms around her.

"You did so good tonight!"

"Thanks, Andrea, you too."

"You want to stay at my place tonight? It'd give us a chance to talk."

"I'll need to get some sleep too."

"We'll sleep. I promise."

"Sure, why not? Do you have a car?" Brittany asked.

"Sure, I always have a car."

"I'll tell my mom I won't need a ride then. She's probably waiting for me."

"You guys only have one car?" Andrea asked.

"Yeah, that's right."

"That must be tough."

"Sometimes it is."

As Brittany continued to remove her makeup, she could hear Andrea in the hall telling someone, "She's staying at my house tonight."

In some ways Brittany felt like a valuable prize Andrea had won. *What if I'd done a bad job tonight?* she thought. She was almost sure she knew the answer to that question. Brittany had seen how Andrea treated people she considered beneath her.

When Brittany asked if she could spend the night, her mother quickly agreed. She seemed glad Brittany had finally found a friend.

Andrea drove her dad's late-model car, and her house was huge. As they drove into the driveway, Andrea used the remote garage door opener. She drove in, and shut the door before she got out of the car. Brittany couldn't help noticing that the garage was bigger than the house she and her mother lived in. There were three cars in there. One of them was an antique Corvette.

"Who drives that?" Brittany asked.

"Nobody. It's my dad's hobby."

"Oh, sure."

"Come on in and I'll introduce you to my family," Andrea said.

Meeting Andrea's parents was kind of like watching a performance in a play. Andrea's dad was an attorney, and her mother was a realtor. They made sure Brittany knew that and mentioned that their oldest son was in his last year of medical school. They were friendly and warm, but Brittany wondered if their acceptance of her wasn't based on how well she'd done in the play that night.

"We ordered pizza for you two. It should be arriving any minute," Andrea's father said.

"Thanks, Dad. We'll probably be in the media room."

"If you watch a movie, choose something worthwhile," he cautioned.

"We will."

"Brittany, you did a beautiful job in the play," Andrea's father said.

"We're so glad you are able to stay over. We hope you'll come back often," Andrea's mother said.

"It'll be easier for her to come over, once their house is finished. She and her mother are having a house built near here."

"Oh, really, where?" Andrea's mother asked.

Brittany felt her face turning red. It was possible that Andrea's mother would know every house that was being built in the area. She could either get deeper into trouble, making up one lie after another, or she could tell the truth. She decided to sidestep the issue.

"Well, actually, the deal fell through, so we're waiting for spring to decide what to do."

"Well, if you need any help, just let me know," Andrea's mother said.

"Sure, we'll do that."

The two ate their pizza while watching a movie off the satellite. Andrea picked it, and Brittany fell asleep before it was over. When it was over, Andrea woke Brittany up, and they went upstairs to her room. Brittany noticed Andrea had a TV and a computer of her own.

A few minutes later, as they were about to go to bed, Andrea asked, "Did you lie to me when you said you were having a house built?"

Brittany was embarrassed. She took a long time to answer. Finally, she confessed. "Yes, I did, Andrea. Sorry."

"Why?"

"I don't know. I guess I was ashamed to be living in a house that's so run down and ordinary."

The bed was huge. Brittany got in on one side while Andrea turned on a night light in the bathroom. When she came back into the bedroom, she said, "I can't believe you lied to me. I thought we were friends."

"Sorry."

Andrea got into bed on the other side. "Megan lies to me all the time."

"Does she?"

"Yes, all the time. I can't trust anything she says anymore."

"What does she say that's a lie?" Brittany asked.

There was a long pause. "Promise me you won't tell anyone, okay?"

"I promise."

"She goes around telling everyone her hair is naturally curly, but I happen to know that it isn't," Andrea said.

Brittany wanted to burst out laughing that anyone would

take that as a serious breach of a friendship, but she didn't because she knew Andrea was serious. "How do you know?"

"I know the woman who does her hair. Believe me, it's not naturally curly."

"Maybe it's kind of naturally curly, but she wants more curl in it."

"Don't try to defend her."

Brittany wished she were home in her own bed. Andrea was supposed to be one of her best friends, and yet Brittany wasn't even sure Andrea liked her that much. *As long as I'm a star, Andrea will be my friend,* she thought.

Andrea went on and on about Megan's offenses against her. The things she listed all seemed so minor. But Andrea had remembered them all.

"Megan used to be my best friend, but after all she's done, she isn't anymore. I hope we can be best friends, but you never should have lied to me about your house."

"I know. I'm sorry."

"I'll forgive you this time," Andrea said.

"Thanks. I won't do it again." Brittany wanted the night to be over. "Good night, Andrea."

"Good night."

Brittany lay in the dark and thought about the friends she'd had in Idaho. Mindy Aldridge was her best friend. She was about five foot four, wore glasses, talked in a little girl's voice, and looked two or three years younger than she really was. Mindy had been her friend for as long as Brittany could remember. They told each other everything, and Brittany never felt as though she had to reach a certain level of performance before Mindy would accept her. They would be friends for life, no matter what happened.

Brittany missed Mindy and the others. None of the kids in Grace had been very flashy, but they'd all grown up together and gone to the same school. Since very few people moved into the valley and not many left, their class had been pretty much together ever since first grade.

Brittany wished her parents had not divorced because then she'd still be living in Idaho. It didn't seem right that on the biggest night of her life, she would feel so alone.

But she did.

3

For Brittany, Friday at school was like one long standing ovation. People she didn't even know kept coming up to her and telling her what a great job she'd done the night before. One of her teachers who'd been at the performance praised her in front of the class and encouraged everyone to be sure and see the play.

In choir, the members of the cast who had solos were again excused from singing. Brittany and Craig went to a room where musical instruments were stored. Their intention was to study, but Brittany was too exhausted from the night before. She kept falling asleep in her chair. Craig was sitting on the floor with his back against the wall. "Want a shoulder to use as a pillow?"

Brittany sat next to him and laid her head on his shoulder. In a few minutes she was sound asleep.

When she woke up, she was embarrassed to find herself practically sprawled all over Craig. Her head was resting on his chest instead of his shoulder, and he had put his arm around her to keep her from slipping down even more. She quickly sat up. "Sorry about that," she said.

"No problem."

"You should've woke me up."

"I didn't have the heart to. Besides, I didn't mind," he grinned.

She slugged him lightly on the arm, then stretched. "I feel a lot better."

"Good."

"How's your studying going?" she asked.

"Well, okay, but I've been having a little trouble myself staying awake."

"Go ahead and study. I'll keep you awake." She opened her backpack. "Guess what I found in the library today?"

"Wow, that's a toughie." He stroked his chin as if in deep thought. "A book, maybe?"

She smiled. "Good guess. But not just *any* book." She showed it to him. "This is about making shadow animals. I think I'll practice now, if that's okay with you."

"Oh, man, you're not going to babble like Mickey Mouse again, are you?"

"No, I won't. I promise."

"Somehow it really doesn't go well with trying to study calculus."

"What's calculus about?" she asked.

Craig shrugged his shoulders. "That's my problem. I have no idea."

"Well, could you just give me a hint?"

He cleared his throat. "Okay, which is steeper, this . . . " He held his hand at a shallow angle. "Or this?" He raised his hand to form a steeper angle.

"The second one was steeper."

"As far as I can tell, that's what calculus is about."

"Gosh, that doesn't sound too hard. Maybe I'll take it next year."

She left the room and returned a short time later, wheeling in an overhead projector. "Don't worry. I'm not going to say a word. You won't even know I'm here."

"I always know when you're around. I have like a sixth sense when it comes to you."

"Yeah, yeah." She flipped on the overhead projector and turned to the first illustration in the book. "Oh, my gosh, Craig, it was so funny when I went to the library to try to find a book on making shadow animals. So, I walk up to Mrs. Netmiller, okay? And I go, 'I need a book about this.' I put my hands in front of her face, like this, to make a bunny. But to her it must have looked like I was going to scratch her eyes out or something. So she backs away and looks at me like I'm crazy. Oh, my gosh, it was so funny."

"Uhm—huhm," Craig said, still trying to study.

Some minutes later, Brittany said, "Look, Craig! I can do an elephant."

He looked up at the shadow figure on the wall. "Right," he said dully.

"You don't seem very impressed."

"Tomorrow I'll be impressed—today I have a calculus test."

"It's a very good shadow-elephant, Craig. Anybody can see that."

He didn't even bother to look up this time. "I suppose."

"Boy, talk about a tough audience." She thumbed through her book. "You want to see me do a swan?"

"Whatever," he said.

She put her thumb under his chin and raised it so he was looking at her. "*I will* learn to do a swan, Craig. And it *will be* the best shadow-swan anyone has ever done in the history of the world. And some day, when I'm rich and famous, you'll come to me on your knees, begging me to do the swan for you, but I will absolutely refuse. Do you want to know why you will get no swan from me?"

No answer. His head was in the book again.

"It's because you're not paying attention to me today. So I just wanted to warn you . . . "

45

"Uhm-huhm."

After turning a few more pages, she saw a shadow figure that broke her up. "Oh, my gosh, this is the best one. I've got to learn to do it. But I'll need help."

Craig sighed. "What do I have to do?" he said, knowing there was no escape.

"Just sit in front of the light, that's all."

She had him face the light on the wall so he'd be able to see the finished shadow when it was done.

She stood behind him and gently lifted two clumps of his hair. Then, after getting her fingers set, she started laughing. "Look up now."

Craig looked up. "What is it?"

"Can't you tell? It's two giraffes eating leaves from a tall tree. Your hair is the branches of the tree."

"Oh, yeah." He turned back to his book. "That's real good," he said mechanically.

"*Good?* Are you kidding me? It's a masterpiece. That's what it is."

"Uhm-humh."

She was standing behind him. It was too much of a temptation. She began styling his hair.

He looked back at her. "Excuse me, but what are you doing?"

"I'm playing with your hair."

"And did I say you could do that?"

"No, not really. But you don't mind, do you?"

"I guess not."

She got her hair pic from her backpack and tried various ridiculous styles. She liked being close to him. Besides, it was fun to give the ever-well-groomed Craig Weston a messed up look.

A few minutes later, he shut his book, then turned around with a sinister smile on his face. "All right, you've had your fun, now it's my turn."

"Class is almost over. What if Diana comes in and catches you styling my hair?"

"I can't go through life worrying about what Diana might think."

"Really? Well, all right then, let's do it."

They switched places. He had a tough time trying to run her pic through her hair. "Your hair is so thick," he said.

"Yeah it is. It's great until you have to get the snarls out."

Craig spoke in a high-pitched voice with a foreign accent: "I tink I vill create sometink quite magnificent for you today!"

"I can hardly wait," she said.

She enjoyed the feeling of having him work on her hair.

While playing with Brittany's hair, Craig said, "Last night Diana asked if I'd be seeing you after the play closes on Saturday night."

"What did you say?" Brittany asked.

"I said I might."

"Really?"

"Well, yeah, why not? We'll still be friends after the play, won't we?"

"I hope so."

"Sure we will." He paused. "I don't know if you'll be interested in this or not, but I've pretty much decided to break up with her."

She turned around to face him. "I thought you two were going to talk."

"We did talk."

"Did you tell her you'd made up your mind to go on a mission?"

"Yes, I told her, and she said she'd support me . . . if that's what I really want to do."

"Then what's the problem?"

"Nothing. Everything's fine," he said curtly.

"C'mon, Craig, level with me."

47

"The problem is I want to spend time with you after the play. I know she's not going to agree to that. So maybe it'd be better if she and I did break up. But not right away. I'm going to wait at least until after her birthday. That's about three weeks away."

"Are you sure you really want to do this?" she asked.

"I'm sure. I need a break from going with someone. I just want to be friends with girls until I go on my mission." He paused. "Actually, I want to be friends with you."

"That sounds good to me."

"Diana will probably think I'm breaking up with her because of you, but it really is something I've been thinking about for a long time."

"If you need someone to talk to right after you break up, call me . . . anytime, even if it's late."

"I will. I promise."

The class bell rang, signalling the end of choir. Brittany quickly got her hair back to the way she liked it and then Craig walked her to her next class.

During class Brittany realized that, if she and Derek doubled with Craig and Diana a week from Saturday, it would be very awkward for her to be with Diana, knowing that Craig was about to break up with her.

When she saw Derek later in the day, she asked if they could go to the movie with someone else instead of with Craig and Diana. Derek told her it would be no problem.

Friday night's performance was even better than Thursday's. After it was over, a steady stream of well-wishers came up to Craig and Brittany, including the principal of the school and also Craig's stake president. Andrea stayed close to Brittany and shook hands with everyone too, even though she had only a minor role in the play. Brittany thought it was kind of pathetic the way she tried to cut in on Brittany's popularity.

She met Craig's parents. They were, in a way, what she would have predicted. His dad was tall, distinguished looking, and charming, but still, with all his friendliness, he managed to keep people at a distance. Craig's mother was much more down to earth and easy to be around. When she came to Brittany, she gave her a big hug. "Oh, my dear, you were so magnificent! Thanks for all the help you've given Craig in the play."

"I didn't do anything. He helped me."

"I think you were both good for each other," she said, continuing the hug beyond what Brittany thought was necessary.

Maybe she really does like me, Brittany thought.

As his parents moved on to others in the cast, Brittany noticed Diana glaring angrily at her while waiting for Craig to be done so she could whisk him away.

Finally the crowd thinned out and Brittany left to change clothes and remove her makeup.

When she came out of the dressing room, she found Derek waiting for her. "You need a ride?" he asked.

She'd planned to call her mother for a ride, but she could see this would be easier on her mother. "Thanks, I guess I do."

He smiled. "I'll give you a ride if you talk the way you did at the beginning of the play."

"Say, Gov'nuh, could I interest you in a flower for your laidy friend? It'll bring a smile to her face. You'd like that wouldn't ya?"

"I love that," Derek said. "Also, I like it when you say, "I'm a good girl, I am."

On the way out to the car he asked her if she'd like something to eat.

She was starving. "Sure, I guess so."

They decided on Mexican. "So, are you looking forward

to our big date?" he asked as they sat down at a table with their nachos.

"Uh huh," she said.

"Me too." He smiled. "Oh, yeah. One other thing. Last week I ordered five new shirts from California. They'll probably be here by then. I'll wear one of them on our date."

"Great," Brittany said, thinking that was an odd thing to tell her.

"I've been thinking of getting my hair styled. What would you think about that?" Derek asked.

"I think that'd be a good idea. There's so much you could do with it. I mean just having it long isn't that great. You know what I mean?"

"Not really."

"Have you ever watched *Highlander?*"

"Once, I think."

"Well the guy who plays Highlander has long hair, like you, but it looks really good on him. I think he probably uses a conditioner every time he shampoos. You can tell someone spends a lot of time on it."

"Would you like it if I was like him?"

She blushed. "I'm not saying that. I just think he takes good care of his hair."

"Consider it done."

"You don't have to do anything."

He grinned. "Hey, whatever turns you on, right?"

She hated it when people said things like that. "Look, I didn't say it turned me on. All I meant was if you're going to wear your hair long, you'll make a better impression if you take care of it. That's all I said, and that's all I meant."

He shrugged his shoulders. "Whatever."

She didn't appreciate his attitude. "I'd better get home now."

"Sure."

When they got to her house, Derek walked her to the

door. She thanked him for the ride and reached for the door. But before she could step inside, Derek suddenly took her face in his hands and kissed her. She hadn't expected it. It made her angry, and she was about to say something, but before she could, he said goodnight, turned, and walked away.

While getting ready for bed, she fumed about him kissing her. He acted like it was his right just because he'd given her a ride home. She didn't appreciate that kind of attitude. *I really don't want to go out with him,* she thought. *But I've already given him my word.*

More than anything, she wanted Craig to break up with Diana, so they could spend more time together. *Hurry up, Craig,* she thought. *This can't happen soon enough for me.*

On Saturday Brittany worked at the mall in the morning, but got off at two so she could get ready for the play that night. It was steady work, but it didn't take much concentration, so she had time to think about other things while she worked. She spent a lot of time mentally going over her lines for the play.

At two she drove her mom's car home. She had arranged to pick up her mother when she got off work at five. They'd eat supper and then her mother would drive her over to the school. It was a pain sometimes, only having one car.

She halfway expected Craig to call. But he didn't. She wondered if Diana had turned him against her.

Around three in the afternoon she took a long shower and washed her hair. Since her mother wasn't around to fuss at her about the importance of saving money, she made it a point to stay in the shower for a long time. It was her way of celebrating. *Some girls party and some girls go shopping,* she thought, *but all I can do is use up the hot water.*

At four-thirty she was dressed and ready. With the house to herself, she decided to say her prayers. She liked to hear herself saying the words without having to worry that her mom would come to the door and ask who she was talking to. That happened once, and from then on, her prayers in her room were almost whispered.

She was in the habit of kneeling by her bed. This time her prayers would not be hurried like so many of them were, especially before school. Her mind was alive, and she didn't get sleepy, like she often did while praying late at night.

She spent a long time on her knees. She thanked Father in Heaven for all her blessings. She didn't do that very often. She thanked him for her health, she thanked him for safety, she thanked him for letting her be in the play and for helping her to do a good job. She thanked him for her friends. She named Craig specifically. She prayed for her friends in Idaho and prayed that someday she'd be able to spend time with them again. She thanked him for her mother's job, which made it possible for them to get by. She thanked him for her talents. She thanked him for her testimony. She thanked him for seminary. She thanked him for being born during the time when the gospel was on the earth. She thanked him for allowing her to be born in America. She thanked him for her job and for her boss who had been considerate enough to reduce her hours during the week of the play. And she thanked Heavenly Father for always being there for her.

By the time she finished her prayers, tears were streaming down her face.

She had so much to be thankful for.

This was the last night of *My Fair Lady*. The cast members had all worked hard to bring the play together. Because this was their last night, she went up to as many people as she could and thanked them for all they had done to make the play a success. Sometimes she gave them a hug. "Let's stay friends, okay?" she said a few times.

She even approached Andrea. "Thanks for being my friend, Andrea. You've been really good to me since I moved here. And tell your mom and dad thanks for letting me stay at your house. I had a good time, and I hope we can do it again sometime."

"Yeah, sure, that sounds good." Andrea paused. "I told my mom and dad how you lied about moving to a better house."

"You told your folks?"

"Yes, why?"

Brittany debated with herself whether to say anything or not. *If I don't say anything, she'll never know how I feel,* she thought. "Andrea, do you ever wonder why you don't have very many friends?"

Andrea acted insulted. "I have way more friends than you do, that's for sure."

"Just listen to me, okay? People would like you a lot more if you weren't gossiping all the time. I feel like I can't ever trust you with anything, because if I told you, it'd be all over school the next day."

"You're in one play and suddenly you think you're the boss of the entire school? Well, you're not, you know."

Brittany shook her head. "I can't even talk to you anymore," she said and then walked off.

Andrea called after her. "Oh, by the way, you don't know anything about a gold necklace, do you? I can't seem to find it anymore."

"I didn't take your necklace, Andrea."

"I didn't say you did. I was just wondering if you knew where it was, that's all."

Brittany walked away, her heart beating out of control. She had never been accused of stealing before.

I need to talk with Craig, she thought. *He'll make me feel better.* She found him with the stagecrew.

"Can we talk?" she asked.

They left backstage and walked into a hallway.

"You okay?" he asked.

"I need someone to talk to, that's all. Andrea just accused me of stealing a necklace from her house when I stayed over."

"Why do you even run around with her? I don't know anybody who likes her very much."

"When you move into a new place, you're glad for anybody who'll even talk to you."

"I'm your friend now though, aren't I?" he asked.

"Yes, but before we moved here I had a best friend. Her name is Mindy Aldridge. We could talk about anything. I miss that so much here."

"You can talk to me about anything, can't you?"

"Not really."

"Name one thing you can't talk to me about."

"I can't talk to you . . . about you."

"Hey, I've been a shadow-puppy for you, maybe I can be Mindy."

They had walked as far down the hallway as they could go. They had come to a steel security door that was locked to keep people from leaving the play and roaming through the school.

"Tell me about this boy you like," Craig said in his imitation of a girl's voice. "On a scale from one to ten, how good looking is he?"

"I'd say, maybe an eight."

Craig stopped walking. "That's all, just an eight?" Craig asked in a girl's voice.

"I took a couple of points off because I don't think he's even shaving yet."

"Are you serious? He shaves all the time," Craig said, in his natural voice. Then, getting back in character, he said in his high-pitched voice, "I heard he shaves all the time."

"Yeah, but I meant to actually put a blade in the razor."

Craig, in his own voice, started laughing. "That is so cruel. I'll shave for you some day. You'll see—I'm going to be a manly man." He spoke in his best Darth Vader voice.

Brittany was already laughing as she said, "Really? When might I expect that to happen?"

Craig threw his arms into the air and pretending to be angry, walked away from her. "I can't believe you said that!" He turned to face her. "I can't believe how bad you treat me."

"I was only kidding, Craig. You know that."

"Yeah, I do."

"Thanks for being here for me. I feel a lot better now," she said.

She came very close to him, hoping he'd give her a hug, which he did. It was reassuring to have his arms around her. "You're my best friend now," she said softly. "You're the one I go to when I feel bad."

"I'm glad for that," he said.

"We'd better get back."

He had his arm draped around her shoulder as they started back. "Oh, by the way, what's the 'magic word' tonight?" he asked.

"Vacuum cleaner," she said.

"Impossible."

"Not really. I'm sure I won't have any trouble putting it in somewhere."

"You're on. Vacuum cleaner it is, then," he agreed.

Saturday night's performance turned into a celebration for the cast. Because this was the last performance, their discipline began to break down. New lines were invented to throw other people off balance. It was not likely that the audience picked up the changes, but the cast did.

At the end of the first act, Mr. Andrews called the cast together. "Look, people, settle down. Do it the way we rehearsed. If this horseplay keeps on, you're going to ruin it for your audience."

The second and third acts went better. But in the final scene, Craig did what he'd threatened to do. After demanding that Eliza bring him his slippers, and as she stooped to put them on him, he reached down, touched her face tenderly, and raised her up. Looking into her eyes, he said, "I don't want a servant. I don't want a maid who goes around running a vacuum cleaner all the time. I want you to be my wife. Will you marry me?"

Brittany didn't know what to say. Her mouth dropped open as she fought to stay in character. Craig put his arms around her, drew her close, and kissed her until the curtain closed.

Brittany was furious. With the curtain closed, she pushed him away.

"What did you do that for?"

"Sorry."

"My gosh, I can't believe you did that without even talking to me about it beforehand."

The curtain opened again. The audience was applauding wildly, and Brittany forced herself to smile and take a bow. She was blushing. To make matters worse, with the house lights on, she spotted Diana in the fourth row glaring at her.

After the third curtain call, Diana got up and walked out of the auditorium.

Because this was their last performance, there was no need to protect the set. The curtain was left open, and people came onstage to congratulate the cast. It was a madhouse for a while. Craig and Brittany stood side by side, greeting well-wishers. Most of the people coming up to talk to them thought the new ending was something the two of them had carefully worked out.

Finally, everyone was gone except the cast and Mr. Andrews. They had work to do. They had to strike the set.

Except for a couple of large pieces of scenery that the school wanted to save, everything had to be taken down and carted out to the dumpster. All the costumes that they'd rented had to be turned in and accounted for.

Brittany purposely tried to stay away from Craig while they worked. She was still mad at him. Finally, he came up to her. "I'm really sorry about tonight. Can we still be friends?"

"Friends? I don't think a real friend would do what you did tonight. Let's face it, Craig, you were hot-dogging out there, and you know it. As far as you were concerned, I was just another prop you needed to make yourself look good."

Craig didn't answer immediately. He put his hands in his pockets and looked down. "You're right," he finally said. "It was a stupid thing to do. I really am sorry."

She wondered if he was just saying that, but she decided not to push it any further. "All right, I forgive you."

"Thanks. Can I work alongside you?"

She sighed. "I guess so."

It took them until nearly midnight to finish and then they went to Mr. Andrews's house for a cast party. They ate pizza while watching a videotape of their performance taken that night by one of the parents.

At first Brittany was self-conscious about watching herself perform. But after a time, she relaxed. She had to admit that, except for a couple of minor mistakes, she really did pretty well. She knew this would be one of the highlights of her high school years and asked if she could get a copy of the videotape. She wasn't the only one. They passed a list and everybody who wanted a copy signed up.

Because Brittany had grown up in such a small town, where she knew every person in her class beginning in the first grade, she had never been treated as someone out of the ordinary. In her school in Idaho, everyone was treated more or less equally, and everybody supported everybody else.

The ones who were good in math helped the ones who weren't. All the boys played on the football and basketball teams. And the natural athletes worked with those who weren't.

Brittany had never thought of herself as pretty, but watching herself on the video, she could see how some people might think that about her. She wasn't sure what she thought about herself. She just was. But in this big city environment, where people were labeled and almost marketed by others as being a certain way, she could see how people might think of her that way. And yet she didn't feel any different. She had always known she could sing, but she had never known she could be the star of a play—or that she was good looking. But maybe she was. It would take some time sorting it out. This was all new to her.

After the video was over and the pizza was gone, the cast was reluctant to end the party. One of the boys had brought some movies, but they were mostly R-rated. Some didn't mind that, but others, like Brittany and Craig, objected to showing them.

"So, what are we going to do?" one of the boys asked.

"Brittany, why don't you show us all the shadow animals you can do?" Craig asked.

The suggestion was not met with great enthusiasm, but eventually Craig talked everyone into it.

"Brittany, go ask Mr. Andrews if he has a slide projector. We can use this white wall for a screen."

When Brittany returned with the slide projector, she noticed some silly grins on their faces.

"What?" she asked.

"Nothing," Craig said. "Go ahead, show us what you can do."

She started with her best shadow animal, a rabbit. "So, what's that?" she asked.

"The scout salute?" one boy said.

"No, it's not that. Here, maybe this will help you." She made a hopping motion around the screen. "You got it now?"

"Oh, I know. It's a TV antenna during an earthquake, right?" a girl asked.

"Oh, rats! That was what I was going to say," Craig blurted out.

Brittany knew she'd been set up by Craig. "No, actually it's a bunny rabbit."

"Whoa, that's a stretch. I never would've gotten that," Craig said. "Do another one."

She did a swan next.

"I know," a girl said. "It's E.T. phoning home."

"No . . . but you're close," Brittany said.

"I know. It's a robot arm from *Star Wars*," a boy ventured.

Brittany came over to Craig and leaned ominously over him. "You did this, didn't you, when I was out getting the projector, right?"

"I don't know what you're talking about. I think the problem is that you're not that good at making shadow animals."

"And you think you can do better?"

He shrugged his shoulders. "Hey, I know I can."

"Let's see you do it then," she said, sitting down.

He went to the wall and stuck up his fist. "Okay, what's that?"

"A wolf!" someone said.

"You got it!" Craig announced, giving the boy a high-five.

"I can see it too," a girl said.

"I can't believe this!" Brittany howled.

"Okay, here's another," Craig said. He took his hand down and then put it back up. It was, once again, nothing more than the shadow of a fist.

"An eagle!" someone said. "No doubt about it."

59

"Right! Good eye," Craig praised.

"Those are so good," one of the girls said.

"It's uncanny, the detail you put into those, Craig!" another chimed in.

Craig turned to Brittany. "I guess when it comes to shadow animals, some people have it . . . and then again, some don't. But you keep practicing, okay? Who knows, someday maybe you'll be as good as me."

She stood up and pointed her finger in his face. "Just you wait, 'Enry 'Iggins, just you wait!'" she said, giving him a line from the play.

They ended up sitting on the couch and the floor in front of it, watching *The Sound of Music*. Brittany was sandwiched between Craig on one side and Megan and a boy on the other side, with a girl leaning against her legs in front of the couch.

While Craig rested his head on the back of the couch, she leaned on him and fed him grapes. She liked the physical closeness of putting each grape in his mouth "You comfy, Gov'nuh?" she teased. "Is there anything more I can do for you?"

"All right!" the boy with Megan said.

Brittany felt herself turning red. "I didn't mean it like that." And it was true. She didn't like to even joke about doing anything immoral and she really hadn't meant anything by her remark. It irritated her how some people took everything wrong.

She and Craig could only take a few minutes of *The Sound of Music*. They ended up sitting together at the kitchen table.

"Where do you want to go on your mission?" she asked. It was the first time a boy nearly her age was about to go on a mission. She'd known boys in Idaho who left for missions, but they were the older brothers of her friends. And now she was old enough that one of her friends was about to leave.

As Craig talked about going on a mission, she saw a side to him she'd never seen before. Namely, his commitment to do the right thing. He wanted to show her something he'd found in the Book of Mormon. Patient Mr. Andrews, who looked like he wanted nothing more than to go to bed, got them a copy to look at.

Craig opened it to Alma, Chapter 26 and began reading. "'We have traveled from house to house, relying upon the mercies of the world—not upon the mercies of the world alone but upon the mercies of God. And we have entered into their houses and taught them, and we have taught them in their streets; yea, and we have taught them upon their hills; and we have also entered into their temples and their synagogues and taught them; and we have been cast out, and mocked, and spit upon, and smote upon our cheeks; and we have been stoned, and taken and bound with strong cords, and cast into prison; and through the power and wisdom of God we have been delivered again. And we have suffered all manner of afflictions, and all this, that perhaps we might be the means of saving some soul; and we supposed that our joy would be full if perhaps we could be the means of saving some.'"

He quit reading and looked into her eyes. "That's what I want to do with my next two years. Going on a mission is the most important thing in my life right now."

"You'll be really good."

"I hope so."

"I'm proud of you for wanting to serve a mission."

"Thanks."

It was two-thirty in the morning by the time Craig took her home. When they got to the door, he put his arms around her and held her. They stood still, holding each other for a few moments, then Craig began to softly sing a line from *My Fair Lady:* "'I have often walked down this street before, but the pavement always stayed beneath my feet before . . . '"

In the play it wasn't his song, but she was glad he was singing it to her.

She kissed him on the cheek then pulled away to go into the house. "I'll see you around, Craig."

"You will. That's a promise."

She went inside and watched through the window as he drove away. Even though it was late, she couldn't get to sleep, so she read her scriptures for a few minutes. And then she said her prayers. She thanked Heavenly Father that she'd become friends with Craig. She couldn't help but wonder if that was the reason she'd moved to Utah.

The next morning her mother tried to get her up for church but Brittany was too tired. She slept until ten and then got ready and walked over to the meetinghouse. She made it to sacrament meeting just after it started.

As soon as sacrament meeting was over, she went back home, ate a sandwich, and then went back to bed. At seven that night she woke up, ate some supper, worked on homework until ten-thirty, then went to bed. She was drained, emotionally and physically.

She wished Craig had called. She missed him already.

4

Monday was a big letdown for Brittany. With the play over, she felt as though she had nothing to look forward to. She saw Craig with Diana in the halls. He didn't look like he was about to break up with her.

Derek didn't help matters either. Just before biology class began, he handed her the movie listings from the newspaper. "Pick any of these you like."

Brittany wasn't looking forward to their date, but she didn't see how she could get out of it. "Who are we going to double with?" she asked.

"Chad Turner. Do you know him? He was on the football team with me. We both played defense."

"I didn't actually go to any of the games this year."

"You should've. He and I were awesome. One game, we put a guy in the hospital."

"How?"

"We both hit him at the same time, me from the front, him from the back. Really messed him up."

"Oh," Brittany said quietly, wondering why anyone would brag about that.

Derek could see she was upset. "It was nothing personal, okay? It just happens. Guys banged me up pretty bad too. It's all part of the game."

"If you say so." She still had doubts about this date. "Derek, there's a couple of things I need to make sure you understand. The first is, I don't drink, and I'll expect you and Chad not to be drinking either. You understand, don't you?"

"Yeah, sure, no problem. I don't drink either."

"Good, I wasn't sure."

"Anything else?"

"My mom will be expecting me home around eleven thirty."

"That early? How come?"

"I'll have church in the morning."

"No problem. You say your mom will be expecting you home early. What about your dad?"

"My folks are divorced."

"I didn't know that. Well, that's something we have in common. Where's your dad?"

"He lives in Chicago."

"Cool. I wish I were in Chicago," Derek said. "Anywhere but here, right?"

"I suppose. Oh, one other thing. You mentioned we might go to your house after the movie. I know this sounds dumb, but my mom is going to want to know if a parent will be there."

"Yeah, sure, my dad will be just getting home from work. No problem. Tell your mom not to worry."

Brittany felt better. "One more thing. It's something else I know my mom will ask. Are you a member of the Church?"

"You mean, a Mormon?"

"Yes."

"Could be. My mom told me once she had me baptized when I was just a baby."

"Mormons don't baptize kids until they're eight years old."

"Well, I'm pretty sure she had something done."

"She could have had you blessed."

"I bet that's it. So does that make me a Mormon?"

"Not exactly."

Derek grinned. "That's what I am then—a 'not-exactly.'"

"Oh."

He laid the newspaper on her desk. "Look, why don't you pick out a movie you want to see."

When Brittany tried to sit with Andrea and Megan at lunch, Andrea shook her head. "This table is taken."

Brittany sat down anyway. "I'm sorry if you're mad at me, Andrea. I didn't mean to hurt your feelings. I'm really sorry." She was never sure how far to go with Andrea. "It's just that I couldn't believe you told your mom and dad that I'd lied to you about us having a home built."

"Why shouldn't I tell them? You did lie to me, didn't you?"

In a nervous gesture, Brittany ran her fingers through her hair. "Yes, I did, and I'm sorry. And then for you to accuse me of stealing your necklace. Do you really think I would do that?"

"I didn't say you did. I just asked if you knew where it was."

"To me that's the same thing as accusing me of taking it," Brittany answered.

"It's not the same thing at all. You aren't perfect, either, Brittany. You said I don't have any friends. Well, you're wrong. I have plenty of friends."

"I know you do, Andrea. It wasn't right for me to say that . . . but I did want you to know how I feel about you being so critical of everyone."

"Nobody's forcing you to eat with us," Andrea said.

"I know, but, come on, can't we still be friends?"

"I think we should let her," Megan said.

"All right, I guess you can eat with us," Andrea said.

"Thanks a lot. Oh, by the way, did you find the necklace you lost?"

Andrea seemed embarrassed. "Yes, I found it."

"Good."

Why doesn't she apologize for accusing me of stealing it? Brittany thought.

But there were no apologies from Andrea.

While they were eating, a few people came up to Brittany and complimented her about the play. She loved the attention, although she tried not to show it for fear of setting Andrea off again.

After Andrea left, Brittany took a long look at Megan.

"What's the matter?" Megan asked.

"Nothing. I just wish you and I knew each other better. When Andrea is around, the two of us sort of become spectators. Even though we're acquainted, I don't really feel like I know you. Who do you talk to when you're having a bad day? I know it's not Andrea." She almost immediately regretted saying that. "Or is it?"

"Andrea and I have been friends since second grade."

"Oh, well that's good, but would you ever come and sleep over some Friday night? We could talk and, you know, get to know each other maybe a little better."

"I guess so."

"Good. Thanks. I'll call you sometime."

Megan left a short time later. Brittany was hopeful that Megan might someday be a friend like Mindy Aldridge had been in Idaho. But that didn't seem likely. A friend like Mindy was rare.

The rest of the school week was boring and predictable. Brittany returned to her job in the mall, working in the food court busing tables. It was a grungy job, but it was steady. One thing for sure, people would always continue to make messes.

She had a mountain of homework from the previous week. Even though her teachers had given her a few days to get caught up, it meant that when she got home at night after work, she had to spend another hour doing homework. She went to bed tired, got up tired, and was tired most of the day. One good thing about her job—it didn't require much thought.

Craig didn't phone all week. The word around school was that he had made up with Diana and they were closer than ever.

The only halfway interesting thing that happened was in choir. Brittany was asked to sing a solo for the spring concert.

On Friday night after she got home from work, her mother was still awake. "I'll be at a single adult social tomorrow night, so I won't be home when Derek comes to pick you up. Tell me what you know about him."

Brittany described Derek in the most positive way possible. He was a "not-exactly" member of the Church, he played sports in school, he was in her biology class, he had gone to the musical, they were going to go to a Disney movie, and they were doubling with another couple. After the movie they'd be going to his house. And, yes, at least one parent would be there.

"I don't like the idea of you going out with a boy I don't even know," her mother said.

"A boy *you* don't know? Mom, *I* don't even know any boys around here yet."

"Can this boy be trusted?"

"He's all right, I guess. I won't be seeing him again though."

"Why not?"

"We just don't have that much in common, that's all."

"I still don't feel right about it."

"Mom, he's already made all the arrangements. What do you want me to tell him?"

Her mom finally gave in.

Brittany wasn't excited about the date with Derek, but she had promised him, and she didn't see how she could go back on her word.

When Brittany woke up on Saturday morning, there were a couple of inches of new snow on the ground. The temperature was barely below freezing, so the snow probably wasn't going to stay around very long.

Brittany didn't need to be to work until ten, but her mom needed to be to work at the dry cleaners at seven. They had worked out a system. Brittany drove her mom to work, then went home for a while before driving herself to work. During her lunch hour, she'd go to the dry cleaners so her mom could take her back to the mall and keep the car. Then, when Brittany got off work at five, her mom would pick her up out front.

During her lunch hour, Brittany went shopping for clothes. She wanted to wear something new for her date with Derek. She bought a pair of jeans and a leather vest that was on sale. Brittany really liked the vest. She thought it would look good if she ever went country line dancing.

She was determined to make the best of the situation that night with Derek. At least they were going to a Disney movie. She knew she'd enjoy that.

Her mother was a little late picking her up at the mall after work, so by the time they got home, Brittany had only forty-five minutes to get ready for her date. She took a quick shower but didn't have time to shampoo her hair as she had planned. After she had worked all day in the mall, her hair smelled like every fast food place in the food court. She put on some perfume, hoping to hide the smell.

Before leaving to go to her single-adult dinner, her mother came in to say good-bye and remind Brittany not to stay out too late.

Ten minutes before Derek was scheduled to arrive,

Brittany was ready. She checked herself out in the bathroom mirror. She sniffed her hair. It wasn't too bad. She hoped Derek wouldn't notice how dry her hands were. Her job required her to wipe tables with a damp cloth, so her hands were constantly getting wet and then drying out. After a day of work, especially on Saturdays, they were often in pretty bad shape. She put a lot of lotion on them to make them look and feel better.

She liked the way she looked in her new vest. Back home in Idaho, the vest would really have gone over well. She hoped to go back to Idaho in the summer and see her old friends. She would be sure to wear the vest then.

She wondered how her mom was doing at the single adult supper. Sometimes she wished her mom would find someone she could marry. Maybe she'd meet someone at the temple someday. Her mother was such a good person. She worked long hours—five days a week. The only days she had off were Fridays and Sundays. She spent Fridays serving in the temple, and, of course, Sunday was taken up with church. She hardly ever watched TV, except for general conference, the Tabernacle Choir broadcast, and some of the programs on KBYU.

Brittany wished she was waiting for Craig to pick her up instead of Derek, but she would make the best of it. At least this would give her practice being with a guy on a date.

Just before Derek was supposed to show up, Brittany realized she didn't have any breath mints. She'd brushed her teeth, but she liked to have them handy, just to be sure that she didn't have bad breath. Not that anyone had ever told her she did. She just wanted to be on the safe side.

She went through her drawer and then her mom's dresser but couldn't find anything. Finally she did what her mom had suggested the last time that had happened. She went to the kitchen and got a couple of cloves. She put one in her mouth and one in the pocket of her western shirt. It was better than nothing.

She got her coat and stood at the door and waited. She was ready.

It's going to be okay, she thought. *Not great, but okay.*

A car pulled into the driveway and Derek got out of the driver's seat and walked up onto the porch. Brittany waited for him to knock before opening the door. It was something her mother had taught her.

"Hi, Derek."

"Sorry, I'm a little late."

Brittany was surprised to see he'd taken her advice. His hair looked much better. Instead of looking like a beat-up old broom, it was pulled back, and he'd put some mousse on it. Tied back, his hair did look a little like the way the star of *Highlander* wore his.

"Your hair looks great, Derek! I mean it. Turn around, let me see it."

Derek grinned. "You like it, huh?" He opened the car door for her, let her get in, and then walked around and got in on the driver's side.

"I really do. What about you? Do you like it?"

"It's okay I guess. It took a lot of work though. I used up almost a whole tube of hair gunk."

"Is that what we're smelling back here?" Chad complained.

"It's not that bad, is it?" Derek asked.

Chad made a crude comment about how bad it smelled.

"It looks great though. I'm serious," Brittany assured him.

"I did it for you, you know."

"Thanks. I really like it."

"I want you happy." They pulled out of the driveway. She expected him to introduce her to Chad and his date, but he didn't. She couldn't believe it. *All right, fine, I'll do it*

70

myself. She turned around. Chad and his date were locked in a passionate embrace.

"So . . . you must be Chad," Brittany said cheerily, ignoring what they were doing.

They broke apart. Chad seemed mad at her for interrupting. "Yeah, so?"

"I'm Brittany."

"I know your name."

Brittany looked at the girl. "And you are?"

The girl gave Chad a glance that made Brittany feel like the village idiot.

"Holly," she said.

"I'm new at school. We haven't had any classes together, have we?" Brittany asked.

"I don't go to school," Holly said.

"Oh, really? What *do* you do?"

Holly smiled at Chad as if she were proud of it. "Nothing."

Right, and I'll bet you're really good at it, too, Brittany thought.

"Why do you care what she does?" Chad snapped.

Brittany stared at Chad for a moment, trying to figure out why he was being so rude, then she shook her head and turned around. She wondered where Derek had found these people but didn't say anything else until they pulled into the same mall where Brittany worked. The two couples got out of the car and walked toward the four-plex movie theater.

The best thing about Chad's appearance was that he was wearing a baseball cap that covered his hair. It was a black hat with purple lettering on the front that read *Colorado Rockies.*

"Are you a big fan of the Colorado Rockies?" she asked.

"Not really. I found the hat."

"You mean *stole* it," Holly snickered.

"I didn't steal it."

71

"Yeah, right," Holly said.

There were four movies playing that night in the four-plex theater. One was a Disney movie, the other three were R-rated. Once they made it past the ticket-taker, Chad said to Derek, "We're not really going to a kiddie flick, are we?"

"That's what Brittany wants."

"Why?" Chad asked.

"Because that's what I want to see," Brittany said.

"That is so stupid," Chad raged. "Let's go to that one," he said, glancing at the sign for one of the R-rated movies.

"I'm not going to an R-rated movie," Brittany said.

"We are," Chad said, pulling on Holly's hand and leaving them.

Derek and Brittany went into the Disney movie. The show hadn't started, and as soon as they found their seats, Derek left to go get them something to eat. When he returned, he was carrying a huge box of popcorn and a couple of large drinks. "I got you this," he said.

"Thanks," she said. She took one bite of the popcorn. It was covered in butter. "You must have got extra butter, right?"

"That's right. Just for you."

Brittany didn't like that much butter on her popcorn, but she didn't say anything to Derek about it. She took small handfuls and ate them one kernel at a time, while Derek snarfed down more than his share.

She felt a little uncomfortable being there in the dark of the movie theater with Derek. She was afraid he would try to put his arm around her, or that he might even try to kiss her again. She figured as long as she was eating, he wouldn't try anything, so she tried to stretch out the time it took her to eat the popcorn and finish her drink.

Once, when he leaned close to her, she spilled some of the drink on his lap. "Oh, sorry," she said.

"No problem," he said, "no problem at all."

By the time the movie was half over, Brittany felt like her face was coated with butter. Also, because she'd had so much to drink, she needed to use the restroom.

"Excuse me," she whispered. "I'll be right back."

"Where you going?"

Somebody needs to talk to this guy, she thought. *That is not a question a guy should ever ask.* "I have to use the restroom."

The restroom was barely clean enough to be used, but at least there wasn't a line. Before going back to the movie, she used a paper towel and some soap from the dispenser to wash her face and hands. She felt grimy. She brought some strands of hair to her face and sniffed. Her hair smelled of stale popcorn. The mirror in the restroom was cracked in several places. By finding a part of the mirror that wasn't shattered, she was able to look at her face. The fluorescent lights in the ceiling put out a constant dull hum, and the lighting made her look a little sick. Actually, she didn't feel very well. She'd eaten too much popcorn.

On her way back to the theater, she glanced outside. It was raining. She didn't know what was worse, rain or snow. Snow at least was white and hopeful, but rain was always a little depressing.

She made her way back to Derek's side.

"Everything come out okay?" he asked.

Just drop it, Derek! she thought. She wondered if she'd ever feel comfortable enough to teach him how to act around a girl. She could help him a lot if he'd let her. The first thing she'd tell him would be to get some better friends, and start getting more involved with church. *He's not a bad person. He just needs some help, that's all.*

Not long after she sat down, he put his arm around her.

"Derek, I'm still hungry. Could you get me another box of popcorn?"

"You're kidding, right?"

"No, not really. It's really good popcorn. Maybe not as much butter this time, okay?"

He looked at her like he wanted to take her head off, but then smiled, and said, "Sure, no problem."

The popcorn got her through the rest of the movie.

The Disney movie let out ten minutes before the movie that Chad and Holly were in. Brittany and Derek waited in the lobby where she watched him play a video game.

A few minutes later Chad and Holly sauntered over to them.

"Let's go," Chad said.

The four of them went outside. It was still raining, and they ran to the car, where Derek opened his own door, got in, and then reached across and pushed Brittany's door open. Then he reached over the front seat and unlocked the back door for Chad and Holly.

"Guess who went through two boxes of popcorn?" Derek asked, as they sped down the street.

"No kidding," Chad said. "And how was you guys' kiddie flick?"

"Real good!" Brittany said cheerfully.

"Derek, you should've been to the one we saw," Chad said. "It was hot. I'll tell you about it sometime."

"Tell him now," Holly said.

"Later would be better," Derek said.

"What's the matter, you don't want to offend the Prom Queen?" Holly taunted.

"Something like that."

Brittany was impressed. *Maybe there's hope for Derek, after all,* she thought.

Brittany had made it a point to bring a watch. She didn't want Derek saying he didn't know what time it was, and dragging out the night longer than necessary.

The time was nine-thirty. In two hours she'd be home, and the ordeal would be over. She doubted if she would ever go out with Derek again, but she had to admit he was trying his best—even though his best wasn't very good.

She thought about what she would tell her mom about the date. Her preference would be to just say, "It was okay." There were some things she knew she wouldn't tell her mother. She wouldn't tell her that Chad and Holly had been in the back seat wrapped around each other when she first got in the car. She wouldn't tell her that to keep Derek at bay she had come up with a clever plan to keep eating all the way through the movie. Her mother wouldn't understand how a boy who didn't even know a girl would want to get close physically. She also wouldn't tell her mother that if she hadn't made a stand, she would have ended up watching an R-rated movie. If she told her mom any of these things, her mother would only say, "I told you I didn't feel right about you dating that boy."

She wouldn't say much about the date. Maybe she'd say the movie was okay. That was safe.

It was quarter to ten by the time they got to Derek's house. In an hour and a half, she could ask Derek to take her home.

The house had been built a long time ago. When it had been built, it was probably the pride of the neighborhood, but time and twenty years of renters had taken their toll.

When they first entered, Brittany didn't see anyone else home, so she said, "Is your dad home yet? I'd like to meet him."

She noticed Chad turning away with a grin on his face.

"I guess he's not home from work yet," Derek said. "He should be home any minute now."

They took off their coats and went into the kitchen. Derek got out a package of nachos, spooned some bottled cheese on them, and zapped them in the microwave.

"What do you guys want to do?" Derek asked Chad and Holly.

Chad suggested they watch a certain video. Brittany had never heard of it. "I know you got it, and I ain't seen it for a while," he said.

"I really don't want to watch that," Brittany said privately to Derek.

"Let's split up then," Derek said. "Brittany and I will go downstairs and play video games, and you guys can watch the video in the front room."

"Sounds good," Chad said.

Derek sent them away with one bowl of nachos and cheese and then made a bowl for him and Brittany.

The kitchen smelled of garbage gone bad. Brittany thought about emptying the trash, but she could see that once she started, there would be no end to the things that needed to be done in that house. The sink was full of dirty dishes, and the countertops were cluttered with things that had no business being there, such as two cans of motor oil— one of them opened. There was a pile of newspapers and a couple of cereal boxes and a partially full plastic milk bottle on the kitchen table.

They made their way down to the basement by way of a narrow, steep stairway and entered a large rumpus room, which was the cleanest room in the house. Even so, it was poorly lighted and smelled musty. There was a well-worn couch and a coffee table facing a TV that had been set up for Nintendo.

Derek showed Brittany his collection of CDs. "Pick something you like."

Brittany sorted through the stack. "Did you clean up down here?" she asked.

"Yeah, I did, just for you."

"Thanks. It looks good."

"I even vacuumed."

"Wow, I'm impressed."

Brittany picked out a CD and gave it to Derek. "This looks good."

"That's one of my favorites," he said with a grin.

They listened to the music while playing Nintendo. Derek was much better at it than she was. After a couple of games, he suggested she practice a few minutes by herself and then he'd take her on again.

She was leaning forward on the couch, trying to concentrate on the video game. He moved over closer to her. She could smell whatever he'd put on his hair. It occurred to her that in the advertisement for the product, the manufacturer might have used the phrase *industrial strength*.

"Sorry about Chad and Holly. They're kind of rude sometimes," he said.

"It's okay, I understand."

He touched her vest. "Is this new?" he asked.

"Yeah, it is. I got it today."

"It looks great. The jeans too."

"Thanks. I got them today too."

"Just for me?" he asked.

"For our date."

"They're not tight enough," he said with a teasing grin.

"They're fine, Derek."

"You didn't say anything about my new shirt," he said.

"Oh, sorry. It's real nice, Derek."

He touched the back of her neck lightly. "It came all the way from California."

She leaned forward to avoid his touch. "You told me."

"You want to see the others?"

"Yeah, sure," she said, trying to concentrate on the game.

"They're in my room. C'mon, I'll show 'em to you."

Brittany shook her head and nodded to the TV monitor. "Bring 'em out. Look, I'm doing better this time. I'm pretty sure that in a few minutes I'll be good enough to beat you."

"Forget it. Nobody beats me at anything."

He went to his bedroom and came out a minute later wearing another new shirt.

She glanced up from her video game. "I like that one too," she said.

"How do you like this?" he asked, taking off his shirt and standing in front of her bare-chested.

"Derek, quit fooling around, okay? Come here and see how well I'm doing now. I'm almost on level two."

He came around behind the couch, she thought to watch her play Nintendo, but instead he bent over her and kissed her on the back of her neck.

"Derek, c'mon, let's play this again. I really think I can beat you this time," she said, trying to steer his attention to the TV screen.

"In a minute. I want to show you the rest of my shirts first."

"If you want to show me your shirts, bring 'em out."

"No, just come in and see them. They're hanging up. It'll take like maybe five seconds. What's the big deal? C'mon, they're really cool shirts. I might even give you one."

He came around in front of the couch and grabbed her arms and lifted her to her feet. "Come see my shirts."

Brittany felt alarms going off in her head. Something was wrong. Derek had become demanding. She felt like she should get out of there.

"It'll just take a minute," he said, coaxing her.

"Derek, let's go upstairs and watch the movie with Chad and Holly."

"It's R-rated. You wouldn't like it."

She knew she'd feel safer with Chad and Holly. "It might not be too bad. Let's just go see how it is."

"Talk dirty to me," Derek said in a low voice.

She was shocked. "What are you talking about?"

"You know, like you did in the play." He was grinning, but it was an ugly, threatening grin.

"That wasn't dirty. That's just the way people in the lower classes used to talk in England."

"Whatever—talk to me that way." He loosened his hold on her arms, but moved quickly to put his arms around her waist and draw her close. He was strong and was pulling her toward his room.

On his way he reached to turn up the stereo. "Do you like this song? It's one of my favorites."

"Derek, what's going on? Why are you acting so weird? Let's go upstairs with Chad and Holly."

"Have you ever played strip poker?" he asked.

"No!" she said.

"You want to learn?"

"No, Derek, I don't want to learn. Let's go find Chad and Holly. We can watch the movie with them." She had begun to panic, and she was almost pleading now. "I won't complain if it's R-rated. I promise. I know I've been hard to get along with tonight. . . . Let's just go up and see Chad and Holly, okay? And if that doesn't work out, we can come back here." Even though she said it, she had no intention of ever coming back downstairs with Derek.

He started to rub her back. "Just relax, okay?"

She twisted to get his hands off her. "Let's go see Chad and Holly."

"What for? They don't even like you."

"Is your dad here yet?" she asked. "You told me he'd be here."

"I guess he had to work late. He'll be home soon. C'mon and see my new shirts. They're all on hangers in my closet. All the way from California. Hey, it'll just take a second."

Brittany looked at her watch. It was ten fourteen. "I need to go home now."

"In a minute. I just want to show you my shirts. They're really nice shirts. In fact I didn't know which one to wear for you tonight. They're all good. I got 'em on sale."

79

"Let's just go upstairs," she pleaded. She broke free and started upstairs, but she had taken only two steps when he caught up with her and once again wrapped his arms around her.

"We'll go upstairs in a minute, but first, just let me show you my new shirts, okay?" All pleasantness had gone out of his voice, and he was now behind her, pushing her toward his room.

Even then, she thought she could humor him. "Derek, c'mon, quit horsing around. This really isn't funny anymore."

He pushed her through the doorway and shoved her down onto his bed.

And then he raped her.

5

Brittany sat sobbing in the car on the way home. At first Derek tried to ignore it, but then finally he slammed his palm against the steering wheel. "Shut up! This is your fault anyway. You never should've fought me, then things would've gone better for you."

She wasn't sure how many times he'd hit her, three or four at least, every time she tried to get free. But then she quit trying. The blows to her head hurt and made her see stars, and she felt as though she was going to pass out. It was useless to resist, and she was afraid Derek would kill her if she kept on fighting.

The popcorn and the trauma had made her sick. "Stop! I'm going to throw up!"

He braked to a stop, and she lurched out of the car and stumbled to the side of the road and vomited. When she finished throwing up, she turned back to the car, just as Derek drove away.

It was still raining, and she was a long way from home. She stood on the curb in the downpour, spitting the sour taste out of her mouth and feeling whoozy.

Derek drove up the road about a hundred yards and then stopped and backed up to her.

He reached over and rolled down the passenger side window. "I could've left you out here, you know."

"I know."

"I should've, the way you treated me. Get in the car."

"I can walk home."

"Hey! I don't have time for this!" He jumped out of the car and came around it after her. "Get in the car and don't give me any more trouble!" He swore at her and grabbed her by the arm and cocked his fist.

Flinching, she climbed back in the car. He slammed her door shut and then hurried around to his side of the car and got in.

As they drove through the rain, he said, "You know you wanted it bad, Brittany, so why not just admit it, and quit putting on this big act." He spoke in an angry voice.

"I didn't want it!" she cried.

"You did. You know you did. You were just begging for it. Anyone could see that."

She turned her back to him and watched the rain run down the side window. She was crying, but except for a few sniffles, she was quieter.

When they came to a stoplight, he reached over and grabbed her by the back of her neck, and pulled her so she was facing him. The mercury-vapor light at the intersection was bright enough for her to clearly see his face. "I'm warning you. You'd better not let your mom see you crying when you go in. You better act like nothing happened so she won't start asking a lot of questions, because if you don't, then you'll be in serious trouble with me." He tightened his grip around her neck. "Listen to me," he said more loudly. "If you *ever* tell anyone about this, I'll kill both you and your mom, I swear it!"

She would never forget the way he looked at that moment. His face was contorted, his teeth bared almost in a snarl, his eyes fixed on hers, as if he wanted to burn his threatening image into her mind. He released his hold on her neck and grabbed a handful of her hair. He pulled so hard that new tears came to her eyes. He made a fist and held it ominously in front of her face.

"I could kill you right now. I could strangle you and take your body to a cave that only Chad and I know about and I could dump your body there. They'd never find you in a hundred years. I could do it right now. You know that, don't you?"

She was too terrified to even respond.

He jerked on her hair. "Say something! Or do you want me to smack you around some more?"

"I know you'll kill me and my mom if I say anything." The words came out mechanically, as if she were a computer programmed to answer a certain way. It didn't even sound like her voice.

He seemed satisfied and released his grip. The light changed, and he started off again.

"Now that's more like it. I just want to make sure we understand each other, that's all. And, of course, I'll see you in biology class every day. And, just by looking at you, I'll be able to tell if you've ratted on me. You know I'll be able to tell, don't you? So don't cross me or else you'll pay the consequences."

His tone became lighter. "But if you don't talk about this, then, hey, we can still be friends, right? It's like they say, Brittany, you got to go along to get along."

As soon as the car came to a stop in front of her house, she opened the door and bolted from the car. Derek immediately pulled away, and she ran into the house. Once she was inside, she took off her shoes and tiptoed into the bathroom and closed the door without turning on the light. She locked the door, then stood there in the dark for several minutes, trying to get control of herself.

She couldn't face seeing herself in the mirror, so she only

turned on a night light. The dim glow gave her just enough light to do what she needed.

She felt as though she'd been shattered into pieces. She ached everywhere. Her left cheek was swollen from where he'd hit her, and her wrists hurt where he'd grabbed them to keep her from getting away.

His smell was on her, and it sickened her. She had to get it off. She wanted to take a shower, but she was afraid of waking her mother, who would wonder why she was taking a shower so late at night.

To clean up, she used the basin and a wash cloth. It was slow work and painful. After she had washed, she brushed her teeth over and over again, but she still didn't feel clean. She was trembling, and every few minutes, a new wave of emotion would come over her, and she would begin to cry again.

The clothes she'd worn were lying in a heap on the bathroom floor—her new jeans and her new leather vest and her shirt and her underwear. They had all been corrupted by his touch. She put on the sweats she used as pajamas, then went into the kitchen to get a trash bag. Returning to the bathroom, she dumped all the clothes she'd been wearing into the bag and tied the top of it into a knot. She carried the bag to her room and stuffed it under her bed. It would all have to be washed, but she would do that when her mother wasn't home.

Almost as a reflex action, she knelt down beside the bed just as she normally did every night before getting into bed. But this time she couldn't pray. All she could do was cry. She wasn't sure if she would ever be able to pray again. She was not clean anymore, not like she used to be. Also, she felt betrayed. How could Father in Heaven have let this happen to her? Why didn't he strike Derek dead?

She was in shock and trembling. She felt as though her life was over and that all her dreams for the future had died—her dream of going to the temple some day—her dream of serving a mission—her dream of going to BYU. All gone.

She didn't want to ever be around boys again. She would never understand what had happened, how Derek could have suddenly turned on her. One moment he was her friend, and then he became a monster.

She longed to go to sleep so she wouldn't have to think, but she couldn't do it because every little noise in the night, every car that passed by, was Derek—coming back to kill her.

Exhausted, she finally quit crying, and mercifully fell asleep.

A little before eight in the morning, her mother knocked on her door and stuck her head in the room. "Brittany, it's time to get ready for church."

Brittany's face was swollen. To keep her mother from seeing the bruise, she turned her face to the side so it was against the pillow. "I don't feel very good," she said. "I don't think I'll go today."

Her mother came closer. "What's wrong?"

"Nothing, really. Just an upset stomach. I guess I had too much popcorn last night."

"I'll get you some Milk of Magnesia."

"No, that's okay. I'll get some later."

"I'll put it by your bed."

Her mother brought in the Milk of Magnesia and set it on the table by her bed. "You didn't wake me up last night when you came in."

"I forgot. Sorry."

"How was your date?"

"It was okay."

"Did you enjoy the movie?"

"Yeah. It was good."

"What time did you get in?"

"Around eleven-thirty."

"I didn't hear a thing," her mom said.

"I just went to bed."

"Did you meet his parents?"

"Just his dad," she lied. "His parents are divorced."

"What's his dad like?"

"He's okay," Brittany said. She had her eyes closed so she wouldn't have to look at her mother.

"Did Derek like your vest?"

"I don't know. He didn't say anything about it."

Her mother looked around the room. "Where is it? I don't see it."

"I guess I was so sleepy I forgot to hang it up."

"That's okay, I can do that. Where is it?"

Brittany knew where it was. It was under the bed in a trash bag. "I don't know."

"You didn't leave your vest at his house, did you?"

"No."

"Where is it then?"

"I don't know. I'll look for it later. Right now I just need to get some sleep."

"You didn't put it in the dirty clothes hamper, did you? Because it is leather." She looked in the hamper. "It's not here. I don't see your new jeans either."

"Don't worry about it, okay? I'll take care of it when I feel better. Why do you have to make such a big deal out of everything?"

Her mother looked at her for a long moment. "You're right," she said. "Well, I need to get ready for church. Are you sure you don't feel up to going?"

"I'm sure."

"Well, all right, I'll finish getting ready. Is it okay if I'm in the bathroom for a while?"

"Yes, go ahead," Brittany said.

Her mother left. Brittany could hear the water being turned on and off. Because of her mother's short hair and minimal makeup, she didn't usually take long to get ready.

In some ways her mother seemed so frail. She only weighed a little more than a hundred pounds. Her marriage hadn't been particularly happy, but at least it had been a marriage. The divorce had taken away their security, and now her mom was the one who had to keep everything going.

Brittany didn't want to tell her mother. She felt that if she added one more burden, it would be too much, and her mother would break. *I need to keep this away from her so she'll never know,* she thought. *I'll just go on like nothing happened. And then everything will be all right. There's no reason why she needs to know.*

She got out of bed and turned on the light and looked at her reflection in the mirror. She'd have to hide the bruise on her face with makeup. It wouldn't be easy to do because she normally didn't use much makeup. She wondered how long it would take for the bruise to go away. Several days probably. She'd have to make up a story that she slipped in the movie theater. People were always leaving messes on the floor, spilled drinks, and candy wrappers. It wouldn't be hard to imagine someone slipping.

She looked for other bruises her mother might notice. There were some marks on her ribs where Derek had punched her when she struggled to get free, but they wouldn't be visible under her clothes. He'd also punched her in the side of the head, but her hair covered that area. Her wrists had some marks on them from where Derek held her, but with a long-sleeved sweater, she might be able to cover them up. No, the only bruise she really had to worry about was the one on her cheek. And she would come up with a story to cover that.

The girl in the mirror didn't even look like her. *I'll get through this*, she thought. *The bruises will heal, the pain will go away. And then I'll go on with my life. All I have to do is get through the next few days. Derek hurt me, but I can't let that destroy me. I have to keep on going. Just get through the next few days. It's not like I'm going to die from this. That would only happen if . . .*

The thought struck her like a thunderbolt! . . . AIDS! She slumped to the floor, leaned forward, and held her head in her hands. Her heart was racing and she had trouble breathing. AIDS! That was a death sentence. Dying of AIDS was slow and painful, and there was no hope. AIDS meant being a burden on your family. AIDS was losing all your friends because they were too afraid of catching the disease from you. AIDS meant growing steadily weaker until, finally, all you could do is lie in bed and waste away. She thought about not even being able to go to the bathroom by herself and losing all her hair. AIDS was a death sentence.

I'm going to die from this, I just know it, I'm going to get AIDS and die. Everyone will know, but nobody will care. They'll say it was my fault.

She was kneeling on the floor with her arms folded across her chest, rocking back and forth. She dragged herself to a sitting position on the bed.

Maybe it's not too late, she thought. *Maybe I can stop it before it gets a hold inside of me. I don't want to die of AIDS. I have to do whatever it takes to protect me.*

She was certain that last night wasn't Derek's first time with a girl. Maybe he'd picked up AIDS from someone else and then passed it on to her.

Suddenly Derek's threat of killing her didn't seem as frightening. If she got AIDS, she'd die anyway. *I've got to take care of myself*, she thought. *I can't let him continue hurting me. I've got to make sure this doesn't go on and on.*

Her mind began coming up with other unseen terrors that might be lurking inside her. It wasn't just AIDS. There were other diseases that people get. Some of them might prevent her from getting married or having children.

Her mind racing, she crawled into bed in case her mother returned to say good-bye on her way to church.

Children. She hadn't thought about that yet either. *I could get pregnant from this.* She'd heard of women having morning sickness when they were pregnant. She'd thrown up on her way home last night. Did that mean she was pregnant?

She knew enough from her biology course to know that it took some time for conception to take place. That might be true about the AIDS virus too. If she could get to the hospital, maybe they could do something to protect her.

But she couldn't see how she could be admitted to the hospital without her mother knowing about it. Once, back in Idaho, she had hurt herself roller-skating. She remembered the red tape about insurance her mother had to go through before the doctor would even see them.

She tried to think of any other way she could get medical attention without her mother knowing. There was the money she had in the bank for college. She could use that to pay for a visit to the hospital. The only problem was that her mother would be taking the car to church, and it was raining. It was a long way to the hospital.

She didn't know anyone who could take her. Everyone she knew would be in church. Andrea had the use of a car, but if she knew what had happened, it would be all over school on Monday. She thought about Craig but knew she couldn't ask him for help. It would be too embarrassing. Megan might help, but she would end up telling Diana, who would then tell Craig.

Well, if she had to, she'd walk to the hospital.

She could probably get the use of the car after her mom returned from church, but it would be noon before that happened. Maybe the process of conception would happen before noon. Maybe it was happening at that instant. She realized she didn't know enough. If only she'd brought her biology book home over the weekend. She needed to study the chapter about human reproduction. She needed to know what she should do—wait for her mother to get home with the car or walk through the rain.

That wasn't her only problem. She wondered how hard it would be to get medical help with no insurance and no checking account.

She could walk. She'd walked further than that before. She could dress warm and put something on her head. It would take her maybe an hour to get there. That would be enough time for her to be examined and get back before her mother returned from church. Nobody would need to know. At the hospital she could say she had a boyfriend and things had gotten out of control, and they'd messed up, and she was there to make sure she didn't get pregnant or get AIDS. They'd probably believe her. She could tell them she'd pay for it on Monday.

She hoped she wouldn't have to tell her mother. It would be too devastating for her. She'd already had so many disappointments in her life. There was no reason to add anything else.

There was just one thing she needed to find out and that was if the hospital would accept her promise to pay the next day. If they wouldn't, then Brittany didn't know what to do. She had money in the bank, but it was closed on Sundays. The money was in a savings account, and Brittany didn't have an account that would allow her to use an ATM machine.

If the hospital wouldn't accept her promise to pay them on Monday, she might have to wait until tomorrow to go to the hospital. She didn't want to wait that long because by then she might be well on her way to getting AIDS, or, almost as bad, becoming pregnant. She felt so ignorant. She wished she'd read more about this in her biology book. For all she knew, another twenty-four hours might be too late and she might be HIV positive by then. She didn't know enough to make a decision like that.

She jumped when her mother knocked then opened the door. "I'm on my way to church. Can I get you anything before I go?"

Brittany turned so her mother wouldn't be able to see the bruise on her left cheek. "No, I'm okay. I just need to sleep, that's all."

"All right. I'll be home around noon."

Brittany said good-bye, and listened for the sound of the outside door closing. She walked to the front door to make sure her mother had gone. Then she went to the kitchen, got the phone book, and took it to her room. Sitting on the bed, she thumbed the pages until she found the yellow pages listing for *Hospitals*. But she had trouble reading the number because she was crying. She wiped at her eyes with the corner of her bed sheet and tried to focus.

Before she dialed the number, she sat for several minutes coming up with the story she'd give over the phone. She'd try to sound older over the phone. She'd say she was from out of town and her daughter needed medical attention. They didn't know anybody so she decided to go to the emergency treatment center. If the person on the other end of the phone asked what was the nature of the care she needed, she'd make up something. It didn't matter because she figured the people who worried about money were not the same people who actually took care of patients.

Finally, she took a deep breath and dialed the hospital's number.

"May I speak to someone in emergency admissions?" she asked, trying to speak in a lower-than-normal voice.

Because she needed good breath support to maintain the voice she was using, she stood up and walked to her window. She opened the blinds and looked out. She had a good view of their neighbor's backyard. It was snowing now, and the ground was covered with white.

"May I help you?" a woman asked.

"Yes, thank you. I'm from out of town, and my two-year-old daughter has taken a rather bad spill down the stairs of the motel we are staying at. I'm pretty sure she's all right, but, I'd like to have a doctor look at her just to make sure. I can get money to pay for it tomorrow, but I really would like to have a doctor look at her today. What do you suggest I do?"

"Do you have insurance?"

"No, but we have money. I can get the money to you tomorrow."

"Do you have a checking account?"

"No, we go strictly by cash back home."

There was a long pause. "Do you know anyone in town who could write us a check?"

Brittany began to panic. "No, it's like I said, we're just traveling through, we're at a motel. Are you saying you won't help my daughter unless I have the money right in my hand? She may have broken her arm. I don't see how you can deny her medical attention when I can promise you we'll pay you tomorrow."

"Are you married?"

"Yes, of course I'm married. How else could I have a daughter unless I was married?"

"Where does your husband work?"

"He works in Idaho. He's a farmer."

"Brittany! What are you doing?" Her mother asked.

Brittany turned around. Her mother was standing in the doorway, looking at her strangely.

Covering the phone with her hand, Brittany asked, "Why aren't you in church?"

"I forgot something for my lesson. Who are you talking to?"

"Nobody." Brittany hung up the phone.

"You were talking to someone. Who was it?" Her mother went to the bed and picked up the phone book opened to the yellow page listing for hospitals. "Were you talking to someone at the hospital?"

"No," Brittany said.

"What were you doing then?"

"It was for a play I'm trying out for. I was just practicing my lines."

Her mother came near to her and studied her face. "What happened to your face?"

"I fell down at the movie theater. Somebody left their drink on the floor, and I knocked it over and slipped. You know how messy the floors get."

"I don't believe that's what happened."

"Well, it's the truth."

"Did something happen to you on your date last night?" her mother asked, reaching to touch the bruise on her daughter's cheek.

Brittany turned her face away. "Nothing happened."

"I'm your mother, Brittany. You can tell me. What happened last night?"

Brittany struggled to keep from crying. She knew that what she had to say would be too awful for her mother to hear. It was better to keep it a secret. "Nothing happened."

Her mother took off her coat.

"You need to go. You'll be late for church," Brittany said.

"I'm not going to church."

"Why not? You always go to church."

"Not today. I'm staying here today. Something is wrong. Please tell me."

"It's too awful, Mom."

"Whatever it is, I want to know."

Suddenly she couldn't hold it any longer. She collapsed on the bed, sobbing bitterly. Her mother quickly sat beside her and caressed her hair like she used to do when Brittany was small.

"Tell me exactly what happened," her mother said.

Brittany decided to tell. The only problem was that, although she knew the word that described what had happened, she couldn't say it. She never watched bad movies. She didn't run around with people who used words like that. She didn't swear. She didn't use bad words.

She sat up in bed, but couldn't look her mother in the face. "I was . . . " She couldn't say it. " . . . hurt . . . real bad last night."

"Were you raped?"

Through tears, Brittany nodded her head. "Yes," she said softly, and then broke down crying again.

Her mother held her in her arms. "Oh, my poor baby, my poor Brittany, how could anyone do this to you?"

Her mother's devastation brought an added burden to Brittany. Now she felt responsible for her mother's sorrow. If only she'd been stronger, then she wouldn't have told, and her mother would have been spared.

"It's my fault," her mother whispered in her ear. "I should've been here last night when he came to get you. I shouldn't have let you go out with him."

They held each other and rocked back and forth and cried together.

"Who were you talking with on the phone?" her mother finally asked.

"The hospital. I was trying to see if they'd let me pay cash."

"Why?"

"So I wouldn't have to tell you."

"Do you think I'd want you to go through this all by yourself?"

"No, but . . . it was so awful . . . I didn't want you to know."

"We can get through this, but we'll have to do it together." Her mother stood up. "Get dressed and get the clothes you were wearing last night. We're going to the hospital."

6

It was still snowing as Brittany and her mother walked into the hospital's emergency entrance. Besides her winter jacket, Brittany was wearing old baggy jeans and an extra-large sweat shirt with a map of Idaho on the front. It had been given to her by a boy back home as a going-away present. She liked to wear it because it was big, comfortable, and still smelled new.

She also wore a baseball cap, because when she looked down, the bill hid her face. She dreaded what was ahead and wanted to be as low-profile as possible.

Her mother knew about hospitals. She led Brittany to Admissions.

"May I help you?" the woman behind the desk asked. She looked tired and a little bored.

"My daughter needs to see a doctor right away," Brittany's mother said.

"What is the nature of your daughter's condition?" the woman asked, sounding a little like a computer-generated recording.

"She was sexually assaulted last night."

The woman looked up with immediate compassion. "I'll get you and your daughter in right away."

"Thank you."

The hospital needed information, which Brittany's mother supplied: name, birth date, social security number, and insurance coverage. Soon they were directed into the area where the medical staff worked. A nurse looked at the admissions form, quickly read the information, glanced at Brittany, and then said, "I'll take you both to one of our examining rooms."

It was a small, well-lighted room, equipped with an examining table, some cupboards, and a wash basin. "You'll need to undress and put on this gown." She handed Brittany a folded-up chalky grey gown and then left, closing the door behind her.

Brittany unfolded the hospital gown and draped it over the examining table. She hesitated getting undressed, embarrassed to have her mother see her bruises.

"Mom, could you turn away please?"

"Yes, of course," her mother said.

Brittany was afraid the doctor would come in while she was undressing so she did it quickly. She put on the gown but it was not much good for covering the back part of her. She had her mom tie the strings. That was better, but still not modest enough.

She dreaded having a man examine her. She had gone to doctors before, but mostly for colds or flu. Even having a doctor listen to her heartbeat had always been embarrassing to her. She knew this would be much, much worse. "I'm afraid," she said. "I don't want a man doctor to examine me."

"I'll be right here with you the whole time," her mother said.

"Will you ask if they have a woman doctor?"

"I'll ask." Her mother opened the door and stepped out into the hall, creating a breeze that Brittany could feel on her back as the door was opened and then shut. She remembered seeing pictures of carcasses of cattle hanging in a cooler while a meat inspector went from one to the other. That's the way she felt.

Her mother returned a few minutes later. "They don't have a woman doctor on duty now. But they did say he'll bring a nurse with him."

Brittany made a face but nodded.

"My feet are cold," she said.

"You can put on your socks if you want." Her mother handed her the pair of socks she'd stuck in her shoes, and Brittany pulled them on.

They waited in silence until a few minutes later when the doctor opened the door. The doctor was younger than Brittany would have liked, probably in his mid-thirties, but a nurse came in with him.

He glanced at the form on his clipboard. "You must be Brittany," he said.

"Yes," she said quietly.

"I'm Doctor Salisbury and this is my assistant, Nurse Anderson."

The nurse smiled. "Actually . . . you can call me Rebecca,"

Brittany nodded. Already she was glad Rebecca was there.

Brittany couldn't help the tears that came during the examination. They just came. It was not that the doctor intentionally hurt her. He was very gentle in what he did. A few times it did hurt, but, more than that, it was humiliating to be examined in such an intimate way.

Brittany wasn't comfortable making eye contact with the doctor. Lying on her back, with her baseball cap still on, she stared at the ceiling and used a corner of a white sheet they'd draped over her to catch her tears.

Rebecca, who was assisting the doctor, noticed the tears.

"Brittany, Dr. Salisbury has a daughter. Would you like to know about her?"

Brittany nodded.

"How old is your daughter, Doctor?" Rebecca asked.

"She's ten years old."

"What's her name?" Rebecca asked.

"Colleen."

"That's a pretty name. What can you tell us about Colleen?" Rebecca asked.

"She loves to clog."

"Imagine that," Rebecca said. "Brittany, what do you like to do?"

"Nothing," she answered.

Her mother spoke up. "She's a wonderful singer. She was just in Fairfield High School's presentation of *My Fair Lady*."

"Really? That's a great show," Rebecca said.

"She played the part of Eliza," her mother said.

"You must be very talented," Rebecca said.

"She is," her mother said.

The doctor looked up from his work. "Brittany, I need to collect whatever evidence I can find. Did you wash yourself after it happened?"

"Yes."

"It would have been better if you hadn't," he said. "It would have given us more evidence."

"I'm sure that was the last thing on her mind," Rebecca said.

The doctor continued his work.

"I never was very good at clogging," Rebecca said. "I tried it once but I couldn't get into the rhythm of it."

Brittany focused her attention on Rebecca's face. She was a beautiful woman, tall, with light brown hair and blue eyes. But best of all was her smile and the way she chattered on about anything, just to divert Brittany's attention away from what the doctor was doing.

"Actually, come to think of it, I'm not even a very good dancer," Rebecca continued. "One time in grade school when we were dancing in class, I stepped on a boy's foot, and he started crying right in the middle of class. Poor guy. I felt sorry for him. It was so embarrassing."

"Why did you become a nurse?" Brittany asked.

"Mainly because I couldn't dance," Rebecca joked.

Brittany laughed, then suddenly began to blubber. *What's happening to me? I can't control my feelings. They're all over the place.*

"It's okay," Rebecca said, taking hold of Brittany's hand and squeezing it. She continued talking about her life, bubbling with enthusiasm and good humor. Brittany tried to focus on Rebecca's eyes and on what she was saying, instead of on what the doctor was doing.

A few minutes later the doctor was finished.

"Rebecca?" Brittany asked.

"Yes."

"I don't want to get pregnant, and I don't want to get AIDS," she said.

The doctor obviously resented his nurse being asked instead of him. He scowled as he said, "I've done some things already, but, also, I'll be giving you several prescriptions to avoid any chance of infection. Please take them according to the instructions on the bottles."

"Thank you," Brittany's mom said.

The doctor was finished with his examination, but he said, "There is just one more thing."

"What?" her mother asked.

"In cases like this we are required by law to notify the police. We've already done that. There's a police officer in the hall who would like to talk to you now."

Brittany panicked. She hadn't thought about the police getting involved. "I don't want to talk to the police," she said.

"It's standard procedure in cases like this," the doctor

said. "You don't want the one who did this to you to repeat it with other girls, do you?"

The doctor didn't even wait to hear the answer. He just opened the door and left.

Rebecca hesitated. "If you want, I can stay here with you," she said.

Brittany was about to ask her to stay when her mother said, "We'll be fine. I'll be here with her."

Rebecca smiled. She reached over and tugged the bill of Brittany's baseball cap. "If you need me, I'll be just down the hall."

As she was leaving, she said, "You can get dressed now. I'll tell the police officer that you'll be a few minutes. When you're ready for him, just open the door."

"I don't want to talk to the police," Brittany told her mother as she was getting dressed.

"I don't think you have a choice."

The comment made Brittany mad. Derek hadn't given her a choice. Her mother hadn't given her a choice. And now the hospital wasn't giving her a choice.

"Shall I tell him he can come in now?" her mother said a few minutes later.

Brittany shrugged her shoulders.

A moment later, a man came into the room. He was very large and looked to be about forty years old. To Brittany he was so imposing he seemed to nearly fill the room by himself. He was wearing a dark blue nylon jacket, brown slacks, and tan hiking boots with yellow leather laces. He had just finished eating a donut, and was making sure there were no crumbs in his dark brown mustache. He carried in a half-empty plastic cup of coffee in his big hands.

"My name is Officer Burton. I just need to ask you a few questions."

Brittany's mother introduced herself and Brittany, who was sitting on the examination table with her legs dangling down and her baseball cap pulled way down to hide her face.

Officer Burton sat down, took a sip of coffee, and set his cup on the floor next to his chair. He opened a tattered spiral notebook. "Well, Brittany, I understand you had kind of a bad time of it last night."

Brittany felt betrayed that the police had been called in without anyone even asking her. She took an immediate dislike to Officer Burton. He was huge, and he was blocking the only exit out of the room. She felt the same panic she'd felt the night before, when Derek had forced her into his room and the only way out of the room had been through him.

"Brittany, did you have a bad experience last night?" Officer Burton asked again.

She answered as sarcastically as she could. "No, it was a real picnic."

"Brittany," her mother scolded.

"Well, why does he have to ask such stupid questions?"

Officer Burton took another sip of coffee. When he breathed, he made a wheezing noise. He glanced down at a report form he was holding. "We need a little information for our records. I hope you understand."

"I'm sure Brittany is willing to cooperate with your investigation," her mother said.

"Could you tell me what happened last night?" Officer Burton asked.

"I went to a movie with this guy, and . . . " she said.

Officer Burton interrupted. "I'll need the boy's name."

"Why? He wasn't the one who did it."

"What?" her mother asked in disbelief.

"He wasn't the one who did it. It was someone else."

"Even so, I'll need the name of the boy you went to the movie with," Officer Burton said.

102

She gave him Derek's full name and approximate age. She said she couldn't remember his address.

"How do you know Derek?" Officer Burton asked.

"From school. We sit next to each other in biology class."

"I see. Alright, go ahead," the officer said.

"During the movie, on my way to the restroom, I looked outside and saw it was raining. I remembered that Derek had left his windows open so I went outside to roll them up. While I was doing that, somebody grabbed me from behind and that's when it happened."

"Do you have any idea who it was?" the officer asked.

"No, it was too dark. I couldn't see his face."

"Brittany, tell him what really happened," her mother said softly.

"Were you there?" Brittany snapped.

"No."

"Then just leave me alone and let me do the talking."

"We'll need all the clothes you were wearing last night," Officer Burton said.

"What for?"

"For our investigation."

"We brought the clothes she was wearing," her mother said.

"You can't have my jeans and my vest," Brittany said.

"Why not?" Officer Burton asked.

"Because I just bought them. They're brand new."

"They need everything for their investigation," her mother said.

"What are you going to do with my vest?" Brittany asked sarcastically. "Give it to your girl friend?"

"Brittany, that will be enough," her mother said.

"It's all right, Ma'am," Officer Burton said. "It's a fair question. We'll look for fibers or hair that we can use for evidence."

"I'll shake it out for you," Brittany said.

103

"We need to send it to a forensics lab," Officer Burton said.

"We'll give you whatever you need, Officer," her mother said. "I had her bring what she was wearing last night. It's all in here." She handed the trash bag to Officer Burton.

"Thank you. We'll get started on this right away." He turned to face Brittany. "About what time would you say it was when you went out to roll up the windows of your boyfriend's car?"

"He's not my *boyfriend*," Brittany muttered, rolling her eyes.

"Whatever. What time was it when you went out to Derek's car?"

"I don't know."

"But that was when you were attacked?"

"Yes."

"Inside the car?"

"Yes."

"We'll need to examine the car to see what we can come up with," Burton said. "What happened after you were attacked?"

Brittany realized she hadn't thought this through carefully enough. She was afraid Officer Burton would catch her in a lie. She needed more time to work out her story. "I went back to the movie."

"You didn't even go to the restroom?"

"Yes, I went to the restroom first. And then I went back into the movie."

"And you didn't say anything to your friend or anyone else about what had happened?"

"No."

"Really? I'm surprised you wouldn't say anything."

"I guess I was in shock."

"And then what happened?" he asked.

"After the movie, I asked Derek to take me home."

"What time did you get home?" the policeman asked.

Brittany wondered what time her mother had gone to bed. "I'm not sure what time it was."

"Well, can you tell me what time the movie got out?" Officer Burton asked.

"I don't remember."

"You told me you were going to the seven o'clock movie," her mother reminded her.

This was getting too complicated for Brittany to keep track of. They had gone to the seven o'clock movie, but she wasn't sure if she should say that or not. Finally she said, "No, we went to the nine o'clock movie." It was a lie, but who would believe she could be attacked at eight o'clock and then spend the next three hours acting like nothing had happened?

"But you were gone from home when I got there at eight-thirty," her mother said.

"We didn't go to the movie right away. We had to pick up Derek's friend and the girl he was with," she lied.

"What are their names?" Officer Burton asked.

"I can't remember."

"I'll ask Derek when I interview him."

Brittany panicked. "Why do you have to interview Derek when he wasn't the one who did it?" she asked.

"It's just part of our investigation, that's all."

At least Derek will know I didn't accuse him, Brittany thought. *Maybe he'll leave us alone because of that.*

Officer Burton wanted to ask more questions, but Brittany said she was feeling sick, so he said he'd check back later. And then he left.

After they were in the car on their way home, her mother said, "I don't believe for a minute that story you gave Officer Burton."

"It's what happened, okay?" Brittany grumbled.

"You don't have to talk to me in that tone of voice."

"Fine," Brittany muttered, determined to quit talking altogether.

A few minutes after they got home, her mother came into her room. "Tell me what really happened," she said. "I know you too well, Brittany. I know when you're lying."

"I don't have to tell you a thing. I don't have to tell anyone."

"Brittany, I'm your mother. I have a right to know what happened to you."

"Look, I'm telling you, Derek wasn't the one who did it."

"Just answer me this—did you go to the seven o'clock movie or the nine o'clock movie?"

"What for? Do you want to play junior detective too? Haven't I been through enough? Just leave me alone, okay?"

"If you won't answer my questions, I'll call Derek and ask him."

"Don't call him!"

"Why not?"

"He's got a temper!"

"How do you know he has a temper?"

No answer.

"It was him, wasn't it?" her mother said.

"I don't have to tell you who it was."

"Did you go to Derek's house after the movie?"

"All right, yes, we did."

"What did you do there?"

"We watched a movie."

"And then what?"

"And then he took me home."

"His dad wasn't really home, was he?"

"I told you he was there!" Brittany shrieked. "Why don't you believe me?"

"It was Derek, wasn't it?" her mom pressed.

Brittany threw her hands up. "How many times do I have to tell you? It wasn't him!"

"Well, if it wasn't Derek, then I'm sure you'll have no objection if I call him and ask what time he took you to the movie and if you went to his house afterwards and what time he took you home." Her mother went into the kitchen to use the phone.

She was trying to find Derek's number when Brittany burst into the room.

"Don't call him! You don't know what he's like! He said he'd kill both you and me if I ever told anyone."

Her mother closed the phone book. "So it *was* him." It was a statement, not a question.

Brittany grabbed her mother by the shoulders. She spoke fast in a high-pitched, terrified voice. "Yes, it was Derek, but we can't tell anyone because if it gets out that we told on him, he'll kill us. He will, Mom, I know he will. So, don't you see, we can't tell anyone. I don't care if he kills me or not, but I wouldn't be able to stand it if he killed you, and I knew it was all because of me."

"He can't kill anyone if he's in jail. That's where he belongs, not out running around looking for new victims. We have to stop him now before he does this to some other girl. We need to call Officer Burton and let him know what really happened."

"No!" Brittany shouted. "Please don't call the police! You don't know what he's like when he's mad. He doesn't care if he hurts people. He doesn't mind at all."

Seeing the fear in her eyes and looking at her daughter's bruised and swollen face, Brittany's mom couldn't stand it. She reached out and drew the battered girl into her arms, holding her close and stroking her hair.

Brittany began to cry again. "Mom, I told him to stop. I tried to get away, but he was too strong. He was so angry, I thought he was going to kill me. After awhile, I quit fighting."

"I know. I know," her mother said, beginning to cry herself.

"There was nothing I could do. I just lay there and let him do what he wanted. I couldn't stop him," she wailed.

Suddenly she drew back from her mother's embrace. "He will kill us if we talk to the police about him," she said, wiping at her tears with her hand. "I know he will. See, the thing is, we can't stop him. Nobody can stop him. He'll do whatever he wants. He told me how he'd do it. He said there's a cave that nobody else knows about. He'll strangle us and then he'll dump our bodies in the cave. I don't care about me anymore," she said, breaking down again, "but what good will it be if you end up dead over this?"

Her mother became angry. Taking a deep breath she declared, "The boy who did this to you will pay for it. If it takes everything I have, he will be punished. He needs to be taught a lesson." Then, looking again at Brittany's bruised face, she softened. "I don't know how he could do such a thing. If he was your friend, how could he do this to you? I just don't understand."

Brittany felt sick. She went to the bathroom and threw up. Her stomach felt as if the popcorn she'd eaten the night before would be in there forever. She rinsed her mouth out and brushed her teeth to get rid of the acid taste.

Her mother came into the bathroom while Brittany was brushing her teeth for a second time. "Brittany, we have to report this. If we don't, then it's just a matter of time before he'll do the same thing to some other girl. Is that what you want?"

She couldn't stand the thought of any other girl being made to go through what she'd experienced. "No."

"Then we have to tell the truth." Her mother started for the phone. "This is out of your hands now. It's my decision. We can't let him get away with what he did to you. He has to pay for this." Her mother picked up the phone and dialed 911.

"Please don't do this," Brittany pleaded through her tears.

"We have to." her mother said. Into the phone, she said, "Hello, I need to talk with Officer Burton . . . Well, can you contact him? It's very important . . . No, there is no emergency now, but it's essential I talk to him right away . . . Yes, of course . . . Well, do you have a number I can call? . . . My name is . . . "

Brittany went to her room and fell down on the bed. She wondered when Derek would come to kill them. If it would be in the daytime or at night. Or maybe at school. He'd come up behind her and strangle her and then he'd dump her body into his trunk and drive to his secret spot and throw her body down into the cave. Even if he was in jail, he'd have one of his friends do it for him.

She heard the phone ring in the other room. Her mother answered it. A few minutes later she came to Brittany's room and knocked.

"Come in," Brittany said.

Her mother opened the door. "Officer Burton would like to talk to you again. He wants us to meet him at the Children's Center in half an hour."

"I don't want to talk to him."

"You have to talk to him. If you don't, then Derek will go unpunished. He has to answer for what he did to you. That's all there is to it."

"Don't you understand what I'm trying to tell you? He will kill both of us if I tell the police it was him."

"Not if I can do anything about it, he won't. Do you want anything to eat before we leave?"

"No."

"Have you eaten anything today?"

"No. I feel too sick to eat."

"You have to eat."

"I will, just not now. I'll eat later."

The Children's Center was housed in a beautiful, old two-story brick home that had been donated to the agency by a well-to-do family. Brittany and her mom arrived first. A few minutes later an unmarked police car pulled in behind them. Officer Burton got out of the car. After saying hello, he led them up the sidewalk. The agency was closed, but he had a key to the front door.

"I'm afraid," Brittany whispered to her mother.

"I'll be there with you," her mother said, taking Brittany's hand.

They went inside.

As they began to climb the stairs, a woman came out of an office to meet them. She had dark, nearly black hair drawn back off her high forehead, into a soft French braid. She quickly took in the situation, her eyes moving from Officer Burton to Brittany's mother and finally resting on Brittany. It was to Brittany that she came. She was tall and slender, and she moved with the grace of a dancer.

"Hello, my name is Julia Gardner. I work here at the Children's Center." She put out her hand. Brittany thought it strange that they would be shaking hands, but it *was* Sunday, and this was a Mormon area, so maybe it wasn't so unusual.

Julia's grip was firm, and she held Brittany's hand a little longer than usual. She looked into Brittany's eyes and said, "We're here to help you." Her voice was soft and pleasant. She was wearing tan slacks and a warm bulky off-white sweater. "What is your name?"

Brittany introduced herself and her mother.

"We didn't expect anyone would be here at this time on a Sunday," her mother said.

"I had to get caught up on some work." She turned to Officer Burton. "Were you thinking of interviewing Brittany here all by yourself?" There was the trace of a rebuke in her tone of voice.

"I knew her mother would be here," Officer Burton said. "Besides, I have to interview her somewhere, don't I?"

"Yes, of course. But, in the future, just call me. I'll come down here anytime, day or night. That's no problem at all."

Julia turned to Brittany. "We usually do the interviews upstairs in the bunny room."

Julia led them up the stairs. It was the kind of house rich families once lived in.

"This is our bunny room," Julia said, opening the door. "Come and see it."

Brittany walked in. The room was decorated like a little girl's room, with light colored walls, lacy curtains on the window, two white wicker chairs, and a daybed covered with a pastel colored quilt and some fluffy pillows. There were at least a dozen stuffed toy bunny rabbits of various colors and sizes arranged on the broad window sill.

"Everyone who comes here gets to choose a bunny to take home," Julia said. "Why don't you pick one out?"

"I'm too old for bunnies," Brittany said. "This is mostly for kids, isn't it?"

"No, it's for everybody. A lot has happened to you. Maybe a stuffed bunny will help you get through this. Look at it this way—it can't hurt, can it?" She smiled. "I don't think you ever outgrow your need for bunnies. I know I never have. But I suppose that's obvious, isn't it? I designed this room. Go ahead and choose one."

Brittany looked over the selection and picked one.

"You can sit there," Julia said, pointing to the smaller of the two wicker chairs. "I'll sit here, and Officer Burton can sit there, on the daybed. He'll have some questions for you. We usually videotape the interview for our records. The camera is kind of hidden because we don't want you worrying about it. The reason we videotape the interviews is because sometimes we need to go over the interview to make sure we have everything. Nobody will see this tape except Officer

Burton, myself, and perhaps the judge who will be assigned your case. Is it all right with you if we tape our visit?"

Let me guess, Brittany thought. *I probably don't have a say in this either, do I?* She would have said it, but there was something about Julia she trusted. "If you have to, I guess it's alright."

"Thank you. I appreciate your cooperation."

Officer Burton glanced at Brittany's mother who was standing in the door. "Actually, it'd be better if you weren't here for the interview."

Brittany was furious about the way Officer Burton had of yanking people around. "Why can't my mom be here?"

Officer Burton rubbed his nose. "Because if she's here, you might not want to hurt her by saying what really happened. She'll be just down the hall. And of course Julia will be here the whole time."

"Fine," Brittany grumbled. "Do whatever you have to do. Let's just get this over with."

Julia reached over and lightly touched Brittany's arm. "I know this is difficult for you. If you'd rather do it another time, we can arrange that. It's whatever you want."

"I'd like to do it today," Officer Burton said.

Julia wasn't all softness. "It's up to Brittany," she said firmly. "This has to go on her timetable, not yours."

Officer Burton nodded. "You're right. Sorry." He turned to Brittany. "Whatever you decide. We can do this tomorrow. You'll have to forgive me. I can be kind of pigheaded sometimes. If you don't believe me, ask my wife." He smiled at his little joke.

Brittany could tell Officer Burton was trying to do better. She appreciated that. "I guess we can do it now," she muttered.

"Good girl," Julia said softly.

Officer Burton stepped out into the hall to start the video-taping system. Brittany's mom kissed her on the cheek and gave her hand a squeeze before going down the hall to a waiting room.

Julia stayed. "I'm really sorry you have to go through this, Brittany, but you know, I'm really proud of you for being willing to talk about what happened," Julia said in her soft, calm voice.

Officer Burton returned and opened his notebook. He sat down and said in his wheezy voice, "Was what you told me today at the hospital the truth?"

Brittany's smoldering anger toward Officer Burton flared up again. She couldn't stand to even look at him. "No."

"Are you going to tell me the truth now?"

"Sure." It was a sarcastic response.

"What is the truth about what happened?" he asked.

Brittany just wanted to get it over with. "I was out on a date having a great time and then I got attacked. Okay? Period. Can I go home now?"

"Who attacked you?"

Brittany felt as though she was talking to a complete idiot. "Derek, my date, okay? Is that all you need?"

She sat rigidly in the wicker chair, holding tightly onto the arm rests. In that position she rocked back and forth, looking at a spot on the floor.

"What happened?" he asked.

"I told you what happened! What more do you need?"

"Can you go through it step by step?"

"Everything?"

"I'm afraid so," he said.

It was painful to go through every single detail. But as the interview progressed, she could see that Officer Burton wasn't so bad. He was trying his best to make it as easy as he could on her, but he had a job to do.

There were some embarrassing moments when she tried to describe what Derek had done to her. Sometimes Officer

Burton asked for clarification, and she had to go over things again. But with Julia's quiet assurance, they got through it.

When it was over, she asked, "What will happen now? When will you put Derek in jail?"

Officer Burton rubbed his nose with his sleeve. "You know, I really wish it were that easy."

"Why isn't it?"

"We have to conduct an investigation."

"I told you what happened. What more do you need?"

Officer Burton cleared his throat, uncrossed his legs, and fastened his gaze on his notebook. He sighed and then looked up. "We can't put people in jail just because they've been accused of doing something wrong," he explained.

"Why not? He said he'd kill me and my mother if I told anyone. I believe him. Does he have to kill us before you do something? That's just great! I should've known nothing would come of this."

Julia, who had been acting mostly as a silent witness, came over and sat next to Brittany. "Brittany, Officer Burton is as good a police officer as I've ever seen. I know he comes across sometimes as being a little gruff. But I know from working with him in the past that he'll do everything he can to make sure that justice is done. You just have to give him a little time, that's all."

"My mom and I don't have time. Derek is going to kill us and dump our bodies in a secret cave."

"Did he say that to you?" Officer Burton asked.

"Yes, on the way home he did. He almost killed me then, but, for sure he will once he finds out I told on him."

"Most of the time when a person like this makes a threat, he doesn't carry it through."

"Most of the time!" Brittany raged. "Well, that will give my mom and me a lot of comfort when we're lying cold and dead, won't it?"

Officer Burton reached out to calm Brittany down, but she moved back. "Don't touch me! Don't ever touch me."

He backed away. "Look, I know this is frustrating, but all I'm saying is we have to be careful. Right now it's just his word against yours. There were no witnesses."

"Are you saying I made this whole thing up?" Brittany asked.

"No, I believe you. All I'm saying is we have to do this as carefully as we can. I'll stay in touch with you and your mom. Well, I guess I'll be going now." Officer Burton stood up, said good-bye, and then left.

"Let's talk a little before you leave," Julia said.

"About what?" Brittany asked irritably. She immediately felt bad about her tone of voice. Julia had been very considerate and helpful.

"The police will do their best to make sure justice is done." She paused. "But there is something you can do that will strengthen the case they have against the boy who did this to you."

"What?"

"In cases like this, when a girl has been attacked, the boy will almost always deny anything took place, or else he will say that it was consensual. That means both parties were in agreement to what took place. However, when a girl has been raped, there are often abrasions inside her that can be used as evidence in a trial. We have something called a video culposcope. It's very small, but it is attached to a TV camera. So if the boy or man on trial claims that it was consensual, this kind of evidence can show that he is lying. We have a nurse who works for us. I'd like you to make an appointment for her to do this procedure. This is your best way to get the evidence you need to convict this boy."

"I've already been examined at the hospital," Brittany said.

"I know, but this gives a visual record that can be used in

a court of law. If it wasn't so important in providing the evidence you need to prove he forced you, I would never ask it of you. But it can help in a trial. I recommend you have it done."

Brittany thought about it for a minute, then said quietly, "All right."

They made an appointment for Monday morning.

A few minutes later Brittany and her mother were driving home. They didn't say much. But when they pulled into the driveway, her mother said, "You need to eat something. What would you like?"

"Cheerios with bananas." It was a favorite from childhood.

"We don't have any Cheerios."

"Why did you ask then?" Brittany snapped.

"Do you want me to go to the store and get Cheerios?"

Brittany knew how much her mother hated to shop on Sundays. "No, just forget the whole thing."

"We have eggs," her mother said. "You have to eat."

"No, I don't. That's one thing I *don't* have to do."

"You never ask for cereal anymore, so I don't have any in the house. I could make you a hamburger though."

"Don't worry about it. Really."

"If you want me to go to the store and get Cheerios, I'll do it."

"I wouldn't want you to do anything against your religion," Brittany said sarcastically.

Her mother turned as if she were going to reprimand Brittany, but then she caught herself and didn't say anything.

As soon as the car stopped in their driveway, Brittany jumped out and ran to her room and closed the door. She still felt the need to get cleaned up, so she decided to take a shower. Grabbing the sweats she used as pajamas, she headed for the bathroom.

"Do you want me to fix you anything now?" her mother asked.

"No. I'm going to take a shower."

"You might want to take a bath. That's what women do after they've had a baby. It helps things heal up."

Brittany didn't even acknowledge what her mother had said. She wasn't sure why she was so angry at her mother or why she resented her suggestions, but she did.

She did end up taking a bath though. And it was better than a shower. She dried herself in near darkness because she didn't want to see the bruises on her body. And then she put on her sweats.

As she left the bathroom and headed for her room, her mother called out, "There're some Cheerios and milk on the kitchen table."

"You went to the store?"

"Yes, of course."

Her mother worked at the temple once a week, and tried to live all the commandments. For some reason the fact that she'd go to a store on a Sunday to buy Cheerios brought tears to Brittany's eyes. "Thank you."

"You're welcome." Her mother kissed her on the cheek. "Don't worry about it one bit."

Brittany sat at the kitchen table and ate her Cheerios with a banana sliced into it by her mother. She remembered when she was little how much she liked that for breakfast, but that was a long time ago.

Such a long time ago now.

7

Brittany didn't go to school on Monday, partly because of her appointment for the examination at the crisis center, and partly because of the bruise on her face. But more than that, it was because she was terrified about seeing Derek again.

She drove her mother to work at seven in the morning and then drove back home and stared at the TV, trying to pass the time. *Daytime TV is so lame,* she thought. She finally turned the set off and just sat in a chair, thinking, until it was time for her appointment.

At the Children's Center Julia introduced her to Shannon, the nurse who was to perform the examination.

"He hurt you real bad, didn't he?" Shannon said as she finished.

"Yes. It still hurts."

"I'm sure it does."

When she got home, Brittany called her boss and told him she was sick and couldn't work that day.

"Make up your mind, Brittany. Are you going to work here or not?" he asked.

"I am, just not today."

"I've been more than reasonable because of you being in

118

that play, but the play's over now, and I need someone I can depend on."

"I know. I'll be there tomorrow—for sure."

"Okay, but if this happens again, I'll have to replace you."

"It won't. I promise."

The next morning her mother woke her up. "Time to get ready for school."

She touched the bruise on her face. "I don't think I'll go today."

"You have to go, Brittany. It may not be easy, but you can't hide here for the rest of your life. Get up and get ready."

Brittany decided she should at least try to go to school. She had missed only one day since ninth grade.

She got up and did the minimum to get ready. Some of the pills the doctor had given her made her feel queasy, and she wasn't sure if she'd be able to make it through a full day of classes and work.

After debating what to wear, she decided on her Idaho sweatshirt, a pair of jeans, and her baseball cap. Some teachers didn't like ball caps in class. If any of them complained, she could always take it off. But the cap was good because it hid her face if she looked down.

Her first two classes went all right. The only trouble was between classes—too many people in too small a hallway. Being close to boys caused her to panic, especially boys who brushed up against her as they passed.

Before walking into her biology class, she looked into the room from the hall. Derek's desk was empty. She was relieved. *Maybe he's sick. Maybe he's been arrested. Maybe he's left town. Maybe I'll never see him again,* she thought.

In case he did show up, she went to the back of the room and sat at an empty desk.

119

She heard him before she saw him. He was out in the hall talking to Chad. They were talking and laughing about something. He moved into her field of vision. His hair was done up the same way he'd worn it Saturday night, and he was wearing another of the shirts he'd bought from California. It was short-sleeved, black with reddish-orange slashes in the shape of lightning.

He sauntered in the room, looked at her vacant desk, then scanned the room and saw her. He strolled back to where she was sitting. He had a bag of M&Ms in his hand. "What you doing back here? You belong up front with me."

Brittany couldn't look at him. She stared straight ahead. She could smell the odor of his hair mousse.

He waved the bag of M&Ms in front of her. "Want some?"

She shook her head. She wanted to run—to get away from him—from his voice, from his smell. She was trying to show no reaction to him, but her body was betraying her. She couldn't catch her breath and began gasping involuntarily. It was a nervous reaction to being frightened that she remembered experiencing when she was a little girl.

"What's that all about?" he asked mockingly.

She shook her head.

"Want some?" he asked again, chuckling to himself as he poured out some M&Ms in his hand and placed them on her desk.

"Just go away," she whispered.

"Well, you can say you don't want any, but I'll just leave some anyway, because sometimes, Brittany . . . " He leaned over and brought his face close to hers. " . . . sometimes you say you don't want something, but you really do, so this way, with the M&Ms, you get to tell me *no* but enjoy it at the same time. Guilt-free enjoyment, huh?" He playfully tapped her nose twice with his index finger. "You see, Brittany, I know you pretty well, don't I? Does that surprise you? I've always known what you really wanted."

He picked up one of the M&Ms and tried to place it in her mouth. She shook her head and turned away.

Laughing quietly, Derek leaned over and whispered in her ear, "What's the matter? Afraid of my germs?" As he turned away, he was chortling at his little joke.

The class bell rang. "Okay, let's get started," Mr. Ence announced. "We've got a lot to get through today."

Derek returned to his assigned seat.

Mr. Ence was taking roll with his seating chart. "Where's Brittany today?"

"She's back there," Derek said. "Not very sociable, right?"

Mr. Ence looked up. "Brittany, I need you to sit in your assigned seat. Could you move up please?"

Reluctantly, Brittany moved up and sat behind Derek.

Mr. Ence finished taking roll and then excused himself to get something from the lab stock room.

Derek turned around and grinned. He leaned close to her. "Looks like you can't get away from me, don't it?"

She refused to look at him.

"How come you weren't here yesterday? We had a quiz. Oh, and also, I took notes if you want to look at them sometime."

She kept her eyes down on her desk. "No," she whispered.

"It's up to you. You know something? You were right about my hair. It's a lot better this way. Just this morning I've had two girls come on to me. So things are definitely looking up for me. And how are things going for you?"

How can you sit there like nothing happened, she thought. *You attacked me. You hurt me. You threatened to kill me.*

"I'm wearing one of my new shirts today . . . all the way from California. Do you like it?"

She kept her eyes on a set of initials someone had carved in her desktop.

Derek leaned close and spoke confidentially to her. "You

121

remember our little talk Saturday night, don't you? About you not saying anything to the cops? You haven't said anything, have you?" His pleasant manner abruptly changed. "Hey, look at me when I'm talking to you."

She refused to look at him.

He continued, speaking quietly, as if he were talking about the weather. "Listen to me. You'd better not have told anyone, that's all I can say, because if you ever do, you, and me, and Chad will do a little cave exploring. And then it'll be your mom's turn. You think she'd like that? I just wanted to remind you, that's all. Have a nice day, okay?" He smiled and then turned back.

Brittany knew she was going to be sick. She ran out of the room and barely made it to the restroom in time. She dashed into a stall, leaned over the toilet, and threw up. It came in waves again and again until she felt too weak to stand. Her heart was racing. Her forehead was drenched with sweat, and she had an awful taste in her mouth.

She couldn't make herself return to biology class. She stayed instead in the restroom most of the class period and then went to her locker. She was at her locker when the bell rang. When she saw a group of laughing boys coming down the hall toward her, she felt threatened all over again.

She dreaded going to choir because she didn't want Craig to see her the way she was now. She didn't even feel like the same person. She couldn't smile anymore, her eyes were puffy, and she found it hard to make eye contact.

She did go to choir though.

"Are you okay?" Craig asked.

"Yeah, I'm okay. I've been sick. That's all."

"Sorry to hear that." He paused. "There's something I have to tell you. I really want to thank you for suggesting that Diana and I talk things out. We finally did Sunday night, and we got a lot of things ironed out between us. She says she's going to support me in my decision to go on a mission.

And we're going to try to be more like good friends rather than the way we were going. So everything's worked out, and I guess I owe it all to you. I just wanted to say thanks."

Brittany knew that meant another of her dreams had just been dashed in pieces. She nodded her head. "That's what I expected anyway."

"But we can still be friends," he said.

"Sure," she said, turning and walking away from him.

The choir was practicing for their spring concert, and Mr. Garcia had them stand on risers while they rehearsed. After they had gone through one song, Mr. Garcia announced he wanted to try something different to see if they could get a more balanced sound. He rearranged the singers and asked Brittany to stand between two large boys. They were jammed together, standing so close their shoulders touched. One of the boys smelled like he needed a shower, and she felt trapped.

She began to panic. Her breathing was shallow and she couldn't sing. Her face was hot, and she felt like she was going to be sick again. Without asking permission, she moved down to the riser below her, where she stood between two girls.

"Brittany, I'd really like you to be where I assigned you," Mr. Garcia said.

She shook her head. "I can't," she said.

"Why not?"

"I just can't, that's all."

"Would some other girl like to be where Brittany was?"

"I'll stand between these guys any day!" one of the girls volunteered with a big smile.

It was better for Brittany between the two girls. She lasted the entire class.

Out of habit, she ate lunch with Andrea and Megan. At first Andrea's chatter was comforting. But then Andrea noticed Brittany wasn't saying anything. "What's wrong with you today?" Andrea asked. "You're so quiet."

"Nothing."

"Are you feeling okay?" Megan asked.

"I'm okay. Just leave me alone, okay?"

"Did you have a good time with Derek Saturday night?" Andrea asked.

"Not really."

"What happened?" Andrea asked.

"Nothing. I just don't like him."

"Do you think you'll go out with him again?" Megan asked.

"No."

"I don't know why you even went out with him. He has a really bad reputation," Andrea said.

Brittany looked up from her tray. "He does?"

"Yes."

"If you knew that, why didn't you tell me?" Brittany asked.

"I thought you knew. Why did you go out with him anyway?"

"Because I thought he was friends with Craig."

Andrea shrugged her shoulders. "Not really. For a while Craig was trying to get him to go to church, but that was a long time ago."

After eating only a few bites of her lunch, Brittany excused herself and left the lunchroom to go to the school library. She found a desk at the back of the room where nobody else was sitting. She browsed through a couple of magazines for something to do.

Her two o'clock class was seminary. She didn't want to face her teacher. Besides, the class had a lot of boys in it. She skipped the class and stayed holed up in the library.

She had missed biology and seminary that day. She knew she needed to do better or she'd never get into BYU.

* * * * *

When Brittany's mother drove her to work, she normally dropped her off in front of the mall. But this time it was different. "Can you come in with me?" Brittany asked.

"What for?"

"I just don't want to walk in there alone, that's all."

Her mother sighed. "If you want me to, I'll walk in with you."

The parking place they found was far away.

"How was school today?" her mother asked as they entered the mall.

Brittany didn't want any hassle about not going to class. "It was okay."

"Was Derek at school?"

"No," Brittany lied.

They were walking down the wide corridors of the mall.

"You can see there's nothing here to be afraid of," her mother said.

"Will you come in and get me after work?" Brittany asked.

Again, a sigh from her mother. "If that's what you want me to do."

"You make it sound like everything is my fault."

"It's just that there's no reason for you to be afraid with all these people around."

"It's all these people that make me afraid."

"I'll do whatever you want me to do. You know that."

"Just for a little while then, if you could come to where I work."

"Yes, of course."

Even though there weren't many people in the mall, Brittany tried to keep busy because it kept her mind from thinking too much.

She always wore an apron provided by the mall. It was

light brown and had the mall logo on the front. She was working hard on one of the tables trying to remove a stubborn stain. And then, out of nowhere, Derek was standing behind her. He grabbed the strings she had used to tie the apron and pulled her into him. "We need to talk, Brittany. Sit down. You need a break anyway. I'm not going to hurt you. We just need to talk." He yanked downward on the apron strings, forcing her to sit down on a nearby chair. He pushed her chair into the table and then positioned his chair behind her. He grabbed her left hand and pulled it under the table so it was out of sight. He squeezed hard on her fingers.

"You went and did something stupid, didn't you? You talked to the cops, after I told you not to."

"No."

"Don't give me that. They came by to talk to me today. Not only me, but Chad and Holly. They're conducting an investigation."

The panic attack from earlier that day returned. Her gasps came uncontrollably.

He whispered in her ear. "I told you to keep your mouth shut, but you wouldn't do it, would you? Well, it doesn't matter. You can't win, don't you know that yet? I've taken care of everything. Chad and I had a plan in case you did go to the police. You want to know what Chad told them? That you were all over me Saturday night, and that he was sure that whatever happened was okay with you. I've got some other friends who will say they've done the same thing with you. So you see, you can't win. You're such a loser, and you're always going to be a loser."

She looked about wildly, seeking desperately for someone who would come to her rescue, but nobody was taking notice of her and Derek.

"I'm going now. I just want you to know I can come and take you out anytime I want—just like I snuck up on you tonight. I can do it anytime I want. And I know where your mother works too. So maybe you ought to go tell the cops that what happened was what you wanted to happen. Because if you don't, it's just a matter of time before I come for you. But, in the meantime, I'll cover my tracks. You just see if I don't."

He took the apron strings and yanked them backwards, and then stood up and walked out.

She raced for the restroom but threw up before she made it. She had to clean up her own mess, and the smell was so bad it nearly made her throw up again.

When she returned to work, her boss said, "Where have you been?"

"In the restroom."

"Ever since you were in that play, I can't get any work out of you."

"I'll do better."

"Have you been crying?"

"No, it's just a cold."

"Brittany, let's be honest here. This isn't working out. I'm going to get someone else."

"No! Please, I'll do better, don't fire me. If I don't work, I'll never be able to go to college."

He sighed. "Brittany, I really am at the end of my rope. I need someone I can depend on. I've been patient, but I'm putting you on notice. Any more problems, and I'm going to have to let you go."

As she worked, she kept looking around to make sure Derek wasn't sneaking up on her. She hadn't eaten much all day, and the smells of the food court were making her sick to her stomach. But she knew her boss was keeping an eye on her, so she forced herself to work hard, even though she felt weak and dizzy.

She managed to last until her mother came for her.

"Where did you park the car?" Brittany asked as they walked toward one of the main entrances of the mall.

"Just outside the door."

"Good."

"Why is that good?"

"I don't want to walk very far in the parking lot."

"Why not?"

"Derek might be waiting for us. He came by tonight and hassled me at work."

She had never heard her mother swear before. "What did he do?"

"He said the police have already talked to him and that he's been spreading lies about me so nobody will believe my story. He also said he can come and kill us anytime he wants. He told me that he knows where you work."

"Why isn't he in jail? That's what I want to know. When we get home, I'm calling Officer Burton and giving him a piece of my mind. If they won't put him in jail, the least they can do is give you some protection. I will not stand around doing nothing while you're being terrorized by that low-life scum. Let's get out of here."

Her mother did talk to Officer Burton as soon as they got home. She told him about Derek's threats. "Why isn't he in jail? He has no right to be out on the street . . . I know you're conducting an investigation . . . but how long is this going to take? I will not have my daughter threatened. I won't put up with it. You pick him up and put him in jail tonight . . . Why not? . . . I don't care about your continuing investigation. All I care about is my daughter is being terrorized by that pervert, and I want it stopped . . . You'll talk to him? Why haven't you talked to him before now? . . . All right, you talk to him . . . but if this doesn't stop, I'll go to your supervisor. I won't stand by and let my daughter be treated this way, do you understand me? . . . Well, all right, we'll see what he does after you've talked to him. Good-bye."

She slammed down the phone. "Officer Burton is going

to talk to Derek and warn him he could be put in juvenile detention if he makes any further contact with you."

"That won't stop him," Brittany said.

"If it doesn't, then we'll do something else."

"What?"

"I'm not sure yet, but I promise you I won't let him hurt you anymore. Tomorrow we'll go to the office at school and get your biology class changed so you're not in it with Derek."

Brittany was aware that her mother was not well enough established at the cleaners that she could just leave anytime she wanted. "I can do that."

The next morning Brittany went to the counseling office. "I need to change my biology class to another hour," she told one of the secretaries.

"It's too late in the term to do that," the secretary said.

"Can I talk to a counselor?"

"I suppose so. I think Mrs. Walker is free," the secretary said.

Mrs. Walker had a small office near the back of the large room. She was a pleasant woman. The framed photograph on her desk showed she had children Brittany's age or maybe a little older. "Come in," she said with a smile. "What can I do for you?"

Brittany just wanted to get it over with. "Well, I've been missing quite a few classes lately, and I just wanted you to know that I don't like to ditch classes and that I'm trying real hard to get back on schedule. And, also, I want to change my biology class to another hour. See, the thing is, if I don't keep my grades up, there's no way I'll ever be able to get into BYU. Also, if I want to go to college, I've got to get a scholarship. That's all there is to it. I've always gotten good grades before. I never ditch classes . . . ever."

"But you're missing classes now?"

"Yes, I missed all day Monday, and then, yesterday, I missed biology and seminary."

"I see. Is there some reason for missing classes?"

"There's a reason, but I can't talk about it now."

"It might help to talk about it. Maybe I can help you solve whatever is troubling you."

Brittany lowered her head. "I don't think so."

"Well, that's up to you, but I just want you to know, I'm always here if you change your mind."

"What about biology class?"

"Who do you have?"

"Mister Ence."

"Let me check." She brought up a computer screen. "His other sections are full. Can you tell me why you need to switch sections?"

Brittany knew very little about Mrs. Walker. It was the woman's first year at Fairfield High, and this wasn't even her permanent job. Brittany had heard she was just there for the year as some kind of an intern while working on a master's degree. She had a pleasant face and a warm smile. She didn't come on too strong, and she didn't seem to be in any kind of a hurry.

"I should probably go," Brittany said.

"Whatever you want, Brittany, but you're welcome to stay if you want to. I'm not that busy right now." She paused. "Really."

Brittany closed her eyes and took a deep breath. She felt like she'd been in the middle of a nightmare since Saturday night, and she was exhausted.

Mrs. Walker's phone rang. She answered it. "I'm busy now. Hold all my calls please." Pause. "I know I have an appointment, but you'll just have to reschedule it . . . I don't know. Anytime tomorrow will be fine. Thank you." She hung up. "Do you want to talk about what's troubling you?"

"Yes, I went on a date with a boy . . . and he . . . attacked me."

"Does he go to this school?"

"Yes."

"Would you like to tell me his name?"

She told her Derek's full name.

"How do you know him?"

"We sit next to each other in biology. That's how I met him, and that's why I need to transfer out of the class."

"I understand. Let's take care of it right now."

Mrs. Walker opened a file drawer in her desk and pulled out a form. She turned to her computer. "Let me bring up your schedule. . . . How about if we move you to first lunch? There's a section with a place in it at noon. How would that work?"

"Great. Thank you."

"Consider it done then. You can start attending tomorrow."

Mrs. Walker patted Brittany's hand. "Is there anything else I can do for you?"

"I don't think so."

"Who knows about what happened to you?"

"My mom."

Mrs. Walker nodded. "Good. How about the police?"

"Yes. They know. My mom took me to the hospital too."

"Excellent. You'd be surprised how many girls keep this kind of thing a secret and try to carry the burden all by themselves. They think they can just go on with their lives, but it doesn't work that way. Will you be getting some help?"

"I guess so. I talked to a woman at the Children's Center. She wants me to see her for counseling."

"It's very important you do that."

Brittany stood up. "Thank you for your help."

"Come see me anytime."

* * * * *

Work that day went better. For one thing, Derek didn't show up.

When she got home, she had something to eat and then started to study biology.

A few minutes later, the phone rang. She answered it.

It was Megan. "Are you okay?" she asked.

"I'm okay. Why do you ask?"

"Andrea was talking about you today. I thought you should know."

"What was she saying?"

"There's talk going around school . . . about you and Derek."

"It's not true."

"I didn't think it was. That's why I called, so you'd know."

"Thank you. Will you tell Andrea it's not true?"

"I will."

A short time later Brittany went to her mother. "Let's go back to Idaho. We could start packing now and be moved in by tomorrow night. Please. I hate it here. Let's go back. At least I have some real friends there."

"How can I move back with no job?"

"There must be something you can do back there. Please don't make me go to school here. Derek's been telling lies about me."

"In time people will see Derek for what he is."

"Don't you see? I can't live here anymore."

"What choice do we have, Brittany? We're barely making it as it is. You'll just have to outlast Derek, and then people will know what the truth is."

"You're not even listening to me!" Brittany ran to her room and slammed the door.

132

Half an hour later her mother asked her to come for family prayer.

"You go on without me," Brittany said. "I don't see that praying does much good for me anymore."

"Prayer always helps."

"Maybe it helps you, but it doesn't work for me."

Brittany dragged the phone into her room and closed the door. She phoned the police station and asked to speak to Officer Burton. The man at the other end said he'd have him call.

The big policeman phoned a few minutes later. "I suppose you're wondering about the investigation?"

"Yes."

He cleared his throat. "I talked to this Chad kid and what's her name . . . Holly. They said they didn't hear anything, and that by the time they came from upstairs, Derek had already taken you home."

"Derek had his stereo on too loud for them to hear us."

"You did scream, though, didn't you?"

Brittany felt a jolt of fear. She didn't know she was supposed to scream. "I told him to stop, and I tried to get away, but he kept hitting me, so after awhile I quit."

"Did you scream?"

She paused. "I don't know if I screamed or not. I was fighting him, though. Isn't that enough?"

"Well, the only trouble is nobody else heard either one of you. So, basically, it's his word against yours."

"What about the physical exam I took at the Children's Center? Doesn't that count for anything?"

"It does, except, of course, it doesn't prove Derek was the one who inflicted the injuries. They could have happened before Saturday night."

She couldn't believe what was happening. "Do you honestly think I would lie about something like this?"

"No, I don't. I'm just letting you know what you're up against if it comes to a trial."

"What are you saying? That nothing is going to happen to Derek?" she raged.

"I'm not saying anything. I just want you to know what you're up against, that's all. There are no witnesses. That means it's his word against yours." He cleared his throat again. "I talked to Derek too."

Brittany closed her eyes. "I can guess what he told you."

"What do you think he said?"

"That I wanted him to do what he did."

Officer Burton sighed. "Yes, that's what he said, all right. How did you know?"

"He told me yesterday. It's not true though."

"I believe you, Brittany. And the medical evidence substantiates your story. So we're still going to pursue this, but I just want you know that it's not going to be easy."

"Nothing is easy anymore. I'm sorry I didn't scream when he attacked me. But if it's any consolation, I feel like screaming now. Just talking to you does that to me." Brittany hung up the phone.

She got ready for bed. She didn't like to look at herself anymore because of a feeling that was growing inside her about what she was really like. The thought had surfaced soon after Derek had attacked her. At first she had tried to bury it in her mind. But it kept coming back.

She'd seen a movie once where a horrible monster lurked in the sewers of a large city. He would come out at night, kill someone, then disappear into the sewer again with the body. Most people in the town refused to acknowledge a terrible monster was loose in their city. That was how Brittany felt. There was a monster living inside her, and she was somehow responsible for what had happened.

Maybe, somehow, she had led Derek on. Although she didn't know what she had said or done, maybe she had given Derek signals. And that's why he'd come on to her.

She tried to think back. The only trouble was that she

didn't know what she'd done to encourage him. She always dressed modestly. But maybe there was something about the way she'd dressed that night. She'd worn jeans and a long-sleeved shirt and a vest, and she'd buttoned all the buttons on the shirt except the top button. The vest and the jeans were new, and the vest was leather. Maybe that was it. The smell of leather. There had to be something. All she had to do was figure it out.

Maybe it was me after all, she thought. *Maybe, deep down, I'm a bad person.* That was her private secret, a fear so terrible that she could never reveal it to anyone. Maybe it was her fault after all. Maybe Derek had been right about that. Maybe that's why he'd done what he'd done.

What could I have done to set him off? she thought. *If it was my smile, then I won't smile anymore. If it was the way I did my hair, then I won't do it that way anymore. If it was the smell of my perfume, then I won't wear perfume anymore. I'll just find out what it was and then I'll quit doing that. I won't talk to boys anymore. That's what got me in trouble in the first place. If I'd never talked to Derek, then none of this would have ever happened. Or maybe it was because he heard me sing. I don't think I can ever sing again. Or maybe it was because I was too outgoing and friendly. Maybe I answered too many questions in class. Maybe that was it. Whatever it is, I have to find it out and then never do that again.*

Something else occurred to her. Maybe it was her long hair. People talked about how beautiful it was. Maybe that was what drove Derek to do what he'd done to her.

Boys can't resist long hair, she thought to herself. *Everybody knows that. Maybe it makes 'em lose control. Too bad I didn't know that. Too bad nobody told me that. If it was my fault, who could blame Derek for what he did? Maybe that's why the police investigation is going nowhere. Maybe Officer Burton sympathizes with Derek because he can see how I could drive a boy crazy. That's why Derek will go free. It's all because of my hair. Well, I can fix that.*

Brittany opened a drawer and took out a pair of scissors. She lifted up a long section of her hair and cut if off. And then another section. And then another.

By the time she finished, her hair was shorter than that of some boys in school.

She would have gone further, but her mother wondered why she was taking so long in the bathroom. She opened the half-closed door and cried out, "Brittany, what on earth are you doing?"

"Nothing. I just thought I'd like a different hair style."

"Oh, my gosh, what have you done?"

"I kind of like it."

"Why did you do this?"

"I just thought I needed a change, that's all."

"Is that the only reason?" her mother asked.

"Yes, of course, why do you ask?"

"Brittany, I'm worried about you. I wish you'd go in and see Julia at the Children's Center."

"I don't need anything. I'm fine, really."

Her mother looked over the damage. "Let me at least make it even."

"All right, but don't take very long."

Her mother spent twenty minutes trying to make it even and then Brittany told her she needed to go to bed.

Brittany went to bed without saying her prayers. Because she was struggling with the idea that she might have been responsible for what happened, she felt guilty and unworthy. *Besides,* she reasoned, *maybe there isn't a God, or maybe he just doesn't care about me.* How else could she explain why he'd let Derek do what he'd done. How could there be a God if things like that happened?

She couldn't sleep. At eleven-thirty she got up and turned on the light. She stood in front of the mirror and looked at herself. *Maybe it wasn't the hair. Maybe it was the singing. Maybe it was being in the play. Derek saw the play. Maybe there's something about the way I sound when I sing.*

She remembered hearing about a man who went into seizures every time he heard Mary Hart on TV. Or was that Kramer on *Seinfeld?* No, it was the actual truth. Maybe her singing voice was like that. Well, that would be easy enough to fix. She just wouldn't sing anymore. She'd quit choir class in the morning.

Maybe it was my fault after all. Maybe I'm evil. Maybe men can't be blamed for what they think when I'm around them. Maybe they can't help themselves.

At least this gave her a possible explanation.

The next day at school Andrea took one look at Brittany in the hall and pretended she hadn't seen her. Brittany didn't care anymore.

While she was at her locker, just before lunch, one of Derek's friends came up to her. "You're the girl Derek fooled around with, aren't you?" His hand was on the handle so she couldn't close her locker. "You want to go out sometime?"

"Leave me alone."

"I hear you like to play poker." He waved a deck of cards in her face. He wouldn't let her close her locker door, so she walked away from him. She knew he might take things from her locker, but she didn't care anymore. Let him take everything. What difference did it make?

The gossip that swept through the school was that Brittany had been the one to suggest she and Derek play strip poker and that she had been the aggressor in what happened. For the next few days, Brittany kept finding playing cards everywhere she turned—taped to her locker and sitting on her desk when she came to class. Some boys flashed them at her in the halls and others left notes on playing cards asking her to go out with them. There were vulgar remarks made to her, and she was humiliated by the laughter that erupted when she walked by clumps of boys standing in the halls.

Brittany began to go to the counseling office to hide out. Mrs. Walker was sympathetic and allowed Brittany to use a meeting room located behind her office as a place to study.

Mrs. Walker invited Brittany into her office one day. "How are things going?" she asked.

"Derek's told lies about me and now they're spreading all through school."

"What kind of lies?"

"That I came on to him."

"Do you think anyone will believe that?"

"His friends all do. My friends too, I think." She told how Andrea had ignored her in the hall.

"I think you should talk to your friends."

"And tell them what really happened?" Brittany asked.

"Not if you don't want to, but you could let them know that the stories Derek is telling about you aren't true."

"I don't have any friends anymore."

"There must be somebody."

"No, not anymore. Derek is the one with friends. He's more popular now than he was before this happened. I'm new here. Nobody knows what I'm really like. They believe any story Derek dreams up about me. He can say anything he wants, and everybody will believe him. All my real friends are in Idaho." She shook her head and sighed. "I hate this place so much. I've been thinking about dropping out of school and just getting a job somewhere."

"I don't think that's a very good idea" Mrs. Walker said.

"Why not? I'm not learning anything."

"If you drop out of school, then that will be another victory for Derek. That's what he'd want you to do, isn't it?"

"Probably."

"He hurt you once. You don't want him to totally ruin your life, do you?"

"He already has," Brittany said.

"It doesn't have to be that way. You can get through this. I know you can."

Brittany laid her head back against her chair and closed her eyes. "I hate my life so much now, everything about it. I hate it all. What can I do to get out of this place once and for all?"

Mrs. Walker brought up her transcript on her computer monitor. "Well, maybe you could think about trying to graduate early. That would get you out of here faster."

"How early?"

"Maybe by next Christmas."

"It would be worth it. There's no reason to stay. I don't have any friends here anyway."

"Well, let's see if we can get you out of here early then."

By the time Brittany left Mrs. Walker's office, she had a plan of how she could finish high school by Christmas of the next school year. It would mean taking some high school correspondence courses through BYU, but it would be possible.

Now, at least she had a goal. It felt good to have something to work on.

Craig had, of course, heard the gossip going around school about Brittany. At first he didn't believe the stories, but then, seeing how different Brittany had become, he began to wonder if they might not be true.

"I think we should try to help Brittany," he said to Diana one night.

"What do you think we should do?" Diana asked.

"I don't know, just try to help her somehow."

"Well, we can do that." Diana paused. "I don't think you should talk to her alone though."

"She's my friend. Why shouldn't I talk to her alone?" Craig asked.

"Craig, I know you always take the side of the underdog, so of course I expect you to not believe the stories going around school about Brittany, but I think you should be real careful about spending time with her."

"Why?"

"Do you have any idea what Brittany was like when she was living in Idaho?"

"No, do you?"

"My cousin knows a guy who used to live near her in Idaho."

"So?"

"She was pretty much out of control there too. He thinks that's why they moved here—to see if she could start over. The things we're hearing about her now aren't that different from the stories that were going on about her back in Idaho."

"I don't believe that."

"You want to talk to my cousin for yourself?"

"Yes."

"He just entered the Army. I'll give you his address if you want to write him."

"There must be a mistake."

"No, there's no mistake. But let me talk to her and see how it goes. Maybe we can both work with her. But let me handle it. You're preparing for your mission, and I'm not sure Brittany is the kind of girl who would be any help."

On his way home that night, Craig fumed about what Diana had said about Brittany. Perhaps Diana was right, though. Maybe he should back off from being alone with Brittany. He and Diana could try to fellowship her together.

The stakes were high. More than anything he wanted to stay worthy to go on a mission.

8

It seemed like a long time to Brittany, but within two or three weeks the stories about her faded into the background. Within a month, the playing cards that boys had thrown in her face to taunt her all but disappeared. Though her reputation had been permanently damaged in some minds, the rumors switched to someone else, and she was left pretty much alone.

She dropped choir. She told herself she didn't have time for it, but that wasn't the only reason. She didn't even like to sing in the shower anymore. Singing brought emotions too near the surface, and she didn't like that. She preferred to be in control.

When a new school term began, she signed up for overload courses. She needed permission, but Mrs. Walker gladly gave her that.

Her life began to take on a certain predictability. She was in class until three, then went to work. She continued to have her mother escort her to the food court and repeat the process after work. It was still frightening for her to be alone in a crowd.

She didn't hear anything about the investigation. After a while she began to feel that nothing was going to happen. That made her bitter. *It really is a man's world,* she thought.

Women have no power. That's why Derek is still walking free. It's all like a cozy little club.

She looked for excuses to avoid church, but it made her mother so upset when she missed that Brittany would go once in a while just to keep her mother off her back. She avoided going to her Young Women's classes though. It was painful when a lesson was presented about chastity or temple marriage. She hated to be reminded of what she had lost. After sacrament meeting, she'd often sit in the car or else on the sofa in the hall.

After a few weeks her Laurel adviser made a special visit to Brittany's home. She asked to see Brittany and sat down with her for a visit. She asked Brittany if anything was the matter.

"Not really," Brittany said.

"I miss having you in class."

"I know I should be there. I'll do better. I promise."

Brittany went to the next Laurel class but had to leave in the middle because the lesson was about the temple. When she got into the foyer, a boy her age came up to her. "I understand you used to go out with Derek."

"I went out with him once."

He flashed her a cynical smile. "I heard all about it."

"What you heard isn't true."

"It's not just one person saying it, you know."

He was staring at her like she was the worst person in the world. She got up and went to the car and waited for church to be over.

It was hard to be in church. She felt isolated. Not necessarily because of an unkind word. Sometimes it was just a glance. It was easy to imagine that people—especially other youth—were talking about her. She had a reputation now, and there wasn't anything she could do about it.

She went twice to the Children's Center for counseling,

then skipped three times, then, because of her mother's encouragement, returned once again.

"How are you doing these days?" Julia asked.

"Just fine. I'm real busy. I'm trying to graduate early."

"Really? Why's that?"

"I don't fit in at school anymore. But that's all right. I'm taking a few home study courses from BYU that will count toward my graduation. I'm also taking an overload at school. That and work keep me busy. That's why I haven't come in lately. But I'm doing okay. Really."

"I'm sure you can stuff what happened to you in the back of your mind for now, but I really think we need to spend some time together."

"Not now. I've got too much to do now."

Julia, sighed. "Are you sure?"

"Really, I'm fine."

"Well, if you won't come in, I have a book I'd like you to read."

"Sure, no problem, I'll read it."

Brittany took the book home, put it on her desk, piled some other papers on it, and never looked at it.

"This isn't a strong case," the district attorney confided in Officer Burton.

"I know that, but we need to pursue it anyway. The boy is guilty. I'm sure of it."

The district attorney looked at the papers on his desk. "The evidence isn't that strong. For one thing, she changed her story. Also, we have a boy her age who is willing to testify she's been promiscuous since she moved here."

Officer Burton shook his head. "He's lying."

"How do you know that?"

"I just do."

"We'll never get a conviction," the district attorney said.

143

"Let's get what we can then." Officer Burton cleared his throat. "I think we owe it to the girl, don't you?"

A few days later, a formal charge was filed against Derek. A court date was set for July, which at that time, was three months away.

For Brittany, every day was another day with no friends to talk to, no joy, no smiles, no music, and very few good times. She focused her energies on getting good grades and working to graduate in December.

Instead of just sitting in the hall or going to the car during Sunday School and Young Women, she began helping out in the nursery. The teachers didn't seem to mind. In fact, they said she was good with children.

On weeknights after work, she would often stay up late working on correspondence courses from BYU. Often she didn't get to bed before two in the morning. And then she'd force herself to get up early. She didn't put much effort into her physical appearance anymore. She kept her hair short so all she had to do in the morning was wash it and then fluff it.

Once, as Brittany was driving her mom to work, her mother said, "I don't see why it's so important to you to finish up early at school. You don't have to work so hard. You need time to deal with what happened to you. The way you're going isn't good for you."

"Why does everyone want to tell me what's good for me? Why can't I be the one to decide that?"

"Oh, Brittany. It's just that I'm concerned about you."

"Just leave me alone, that's all I want. As soon as I graduate, then I'll clear out and I won't be in your way anymore. You can live in your fantasy world, go to the temple, and not be bothered by me. That's what you want, isn't it?"

Her mother looked as though she were going to cry.

"No, that's not what I want. I want you back the way you were."

"It's too late for that now." Brittany felt bad, but there wasn't anything she could do about it.

Brittany was relieved when school finally ended for the summer. She continued working at the food court in the mall, but she also got a second job, working at a brand new Burger King not far from her home. She'd met the new manager at the food court. He'd been impressed by what a hard worker she was and had offered her the job. That meant that between the two jobs she was working around fifty hours a week. She often had to work Sundays, but that didn't bother her much anymore. She didn't really have any friends at church anyway.

Nothing could have prepared Brittany for the court hearing. The courtroom was small. Derek hardly looked like the same person. His long hair had been cut off and he was sporting a regular, short haircut. He was wearing a tie and a sports jacket with some nice slacks. Derek's father was there, along with two of Derek's friends, who were also wearing ties and jackets. They sat in the front row, behind Derek and his attorney. Brittany's mother sat directly behind her.

When the judge entered the courtroom, everyone stood until he told them to be seated, and the case was immediately called by the clerk of the court. As soon as that happened, Derek's attorney asked for a conference between the lawyers and the judge.

Brittany sat and watched as the two attorneys huddled with the judge in front of the judge's podium. She was anxious to testify, and she wondered what was being said. At first she had been fearful about facing Derek in court, but now she was ready to tell her story and see to it that he got the punishment he deserved. She wanted Derek to have to face up to what he'd done to her. She wanted to see him squirm. And in the end she wanted him locked up for a long time. That's what she wanted.

What she got was the judge and the two lawyers talking in muted tones in front of the bench. She wasn't sure what was going on, but whatever it was, it didn't seem to involve her. She couldn't even hear what they were saying.

It ended when the district attorney said, "We'll accept that."

"Accept what?" Brittany asked timidly when he sat down next to her.

"We've come up with a plea agreement. It's the best I could do, believe me. This was never a strong case. I've learned you only fight the cases you think you can win. This wasn't one of them."

The judge had Derek stand as he read the plea bargain sentence. Derek would be on probation for a year, and he would have to undergo counseling.

The judge banged his gavel. Derek turned around to his friends and gave each of them a high five. He then turned to face Brittany and gave a triumphant smirk in her direction. He and his father hugged, then left the courtroom with their arms around each other's shoulders. The attorney and the district attorney talked briefly as they packed their brief cases. And then they also left.

The judge came down from the bench and walked over to where she and her mom were seated, too stunned to move. "May I speak to you and your mother in my chambers? Just follow me, please."

They went with him into a small office just off the courtroom.

"I usually don't do this, but I feel like I need to say something. I'm sorry this didn't work out any better for the two of you. If it's any consolation, I believe the boy was guilty, but the district attorney didn't think there was sufficient evidence to convict him. At least this way, there are some consequences."

Brittany couldn't say anything. She was still in shock. She dropped her head and looked down at the floor.

"Thank you for talking to us," her mom said.

"I'm sorry. Sometimes the system doesn't work perfectly."

Brittany was worried she might throw up. Without saying anything, she turned and walked out of the office. She stumbled down the hall looking for a restroom. *It wasn't just that night,* she thought. *Derek is still hurting me. I couldn't stop him that night, and I still can't stop him.*

She felt an uncontrollable rage growing inside of her. She hated it that her mother was still talking to the judge, trying to smooth things over, excusing her daughter's bad manners in just walking out. She was probably explaining that her daughter had been taught better. Maybe she was thanking the judge for all he had done, when all he had done was to say, in effect, that it was all right what Derek had done—that boys will be boys. Or maybe the message was that if Brittany had screamed or not changed her story, things would have turned out differently.

She finally found a restroom. She entered a stall, got down on her knees, but nothing would come. Frustration washed over her, and she rested her head on her arm and sobbed. It was a tiled room with a high ceiling and the sounds echoed back at her. She wondered if anyone could hear, but then she decided she didn't care anymore. She didn't care if she got her new dress soiled. The district attorney had recommended she wear a nice dress to impress the judge, but she couldn't see what good it had done.

Her mother found her in the restroom. She tried to comfort Brittany. "I know this isn't what we wanted, but we'll just have to live with it."

Live with it, she thought. *I've lived with it since it*

happened. That's all I've done, is live with it. How can they let him walk away after what he did to me? What is wrong with these people?

"We can't stay here. Let's go home."

Brittany walked with her mother to the car. Once they got home, Brittany went into her room and closed the door. She wanted to scream, but she didn't do it because she knew, if she did, her mother would come.

She stood by her bed. She was beyond tears. She felt like the top of her head was about to blow up. Things never got better for her. But, at the same time, Derek always skated free.

As she changed clothes, she found herself staring at the new dress she'd worn for the trial. She remembered how much effort she and her mother had put into finding just the right dress so her testimony would be believed.

What good had the dress done? She had worn it half an hour while three men, strangers to her, horse-traded over the court case. In the end, they decided to make it easy on Derek. *Poor Derek.*

She got the scissors from the kitchen drawer, returned to her room, shut the door, then hacked the dress into pieces. She ended up kneeling over the dress, stabbing the remnants with her scissors, and sobbing.

Hearing Brittany cry, her mother rushed to her room. "Oh, Brittany!"

Still kneeling over the dress, holding the scissors, Brittany turned to her mother. "I can't stand this anymore! If you don't get me some help soon, I'm going to kill myself."

Her mother knelt down beside her, carefully removed the scissors, then held Brittany in her arms. "It's okay, Baby. It's okay. We'll get you the help you need. Come with me. Let's get in the car. It's going to be okay. We'll find someone to help you."

148

"Why doesn't it get better?" Brittany cried out. "I can't stand it anymore." Her sobs, now uncontrollable, shook her body.

"C'mon, Baby, come with me. That's it. That's my big girl."

Slowly, mother and daughter made their way out to the car.

9

Julia Gardner, the counselor at the Children's Center, was at home when Brittany's mother called and asked if they could see her right away. She said she could be there in half an hour.

Brittany and her mother arrived before Julia. They sat waiting in the car. "How about if we drive around for a while?" Brittany asked.

"We really can't afford to waste the gas. We'll be fine here, don't you think?"

Brittany was restless. "Can we take a walk then?"

"Of course, if that's what you'd like."

They walked around the block once and then Julia showed up.

Julia and Brittany ended up in the bunny room, just like the first time Brittany had come.

"What can I do to help you?" Julia asked after closing the door and sitting down across from Brittany.

"I feel like I'm losing it," Brittany said.

"What's happened?"

"Well, for one thing, Derek's so-called trial was a joke. Basically he gets a slap on his hand and then goes free. That is so unfair."

"What do you want me to do?" Julia asked.

Brittany's shoulders slumped. "I don't know. There's probably nothing you can do. I guess I'm just a hopeless case."

"Can I say something you probably don't want to hear?" Julia said.

"I guess."

"You can't recover from a rape without counseling. Why did you quit coming to see me?"

"I got busy, besides, I was doing okay for a while."

"That's just because you were trying to ignore it."

"What's wrong with that?" Brittany asked.

"What happened to you can't be ignored. You can't pretend it never happened. You have to bring it out in the open and talk about it. It doesn't have to be with me. But you have to talk about it. The sooner you do it, the sooner you'll be able to get on with your life."

"Talking about it won't change what happened."

"No, but it will give you a chance to vent your feelings and get the anger out and heal. Brittany, you were violated, and it takes an effort to get over that. You can't just ignore it and hope it will go away.

"Think of it this way. It's like climbing a mountain. You can't just stand at the bottom and wish you were on top. You have to make the climb. Once you've made it to the top, then you have a clear perspective. When you first start, you can't see much of what's around you, but after you get to the top, then you can see things more clearly. That's what we need to have happen. We need to get you on the top of the mountain."

Brittany liked the way Julia talked, soft and quiet and calm. She felt better just being there. "How long would counseling take?" she asked.

"That's hard to say. It depends how hard you work at it, and how willing you are to trust me. It's not easy. Some of what we talk about will be painful, but when it's over, you won't have this coming back to haunt you in ten or fifteen years. The time to take care of this is right now."

"How often would I have to come?" Brittany asked.

"That's up to you. I'd say maybe two or three times a week to begin with and then maybe once a week after that."

"I'm not sure it's worth your time."

"Believe me, it is. You're very important to me. I will never abandon you, no matter what happens."

Brittany did not mean to cry, but she did, and for a long time. There, curled up on the white wicker sofa, surrounded by white and pink and gray bunnies, she sobbed until the bunny she was holding was soaked. While Brittany cried, Julia waited patiently.

"You probably need to get home to your family, don't you?" Brittany finally said, drying her face with the sleeve of her shirt.

"I'm fine, really."

"I don't see why you waste your time with me."

"Because you're important to me."

Brittany decided she should get it out up front, in case Julia would change her mind. "There's something you should know."

"What's that?"

She could barely say it. "I think I made it happen."

Julia leaned closer so she could hear better. "Made what happen?"

"What Derek did to me," she whispered, not daring to look Julia in the face.

"How did you make it happen?" Julia asked.

"I don't know. When Derek took me home, he told me he knew I'd wanted it."

"Did you tell him that beforehand?"

"No, but somehow he knew. There's something about me that turned him on."

"*Did* you want it to happen?"

Brittany shook her head. "No!"

"Then why do you think you made it happen?"

"There must have been something I said, or maybe I wore the wrong clothes."

"It doesn't matter what you wore," Julia said.

"How can you say it doesn't matter? In church they tell us to be careful what we wear. Why would they tell us that if it doesn't matter?"

"When he first grabbed you, did you tell him to stop?" Julia asked.

"Yes, at first, but then, later, after he started hitting me, I was afraid to say anything."

Julia moved her chair close enough to touch Brittany on the chin and raise her head so there was eye contact between them. "Listen to me, Brittany—no means *no!* It doesn't matter what you wore or what you said beforehand. When you say no, you mean no."

Brittany closed her eyes and shook her head. "But there must have been something I did."

"Why must there be?" Julia asked.

"I don't know why."

"It wasn't something you did."

"How do you know? You weren't there."

"If what you've told me is the truth, you did nothing to cause this. You were the victim of an act of violence."

"I must have done something though."

"He attacked you, didn't he?" Julia asked.

"Yes."

"Whoever he'd been with that night, he would have done the same thing."

"What if I'd worn tight jeans and a tank top? Would it still be his fault?"

"Yes."

Brittany sat with her arms folded tightly around her, her

head down. "What if I'd led him along, kissed him a lot of times, and then changed my mind?"

"What he does after you say no is his responsibility. You have a right to say what happens. When it's against your will, then it's his fault."

"I shouldn't have gone out with him."

"That may be true, but you had no reason to suspect him, did you?"

"No. Not really."

"Brittany, it's quite likely he planned this from the very beginning. I would guess he's done this before. You were not the first, and, unless his counseling takes hold, you may not be the last. This kind of violence doesn't come out of nowhere. It was acted out in his mind long before he met you. I am certain this didn't happen because of what you wore or said that night."

"But what if a guy sees a girl and gets turned on and can't stop himself?"

"A man can always stop. Besides, what he did to you isn't about sex. It's about exerting power over someone. That's what he wanted. He wanted to take away your right to make a choice. Rape is an act of violence. It's not about passion or what perfume you wore or if you smiled a certain way or how tight your jeans were. It's about one person try- ing to make another person powerless. You were a victim, Brittany, just as much as if you stepped off the curb and were hit by a speeding car.

"It could have been any girl that night. Someone taller, someone shorter, someone with different colored hair. It wouldn't have made any difference. It wasn't that you did something wrong. He was the one who did something wrong. Not you. You can't blame yourself. He is the one to blame because he is the one who did this to you against your will. If you're going to get mad at someone, get mad at

154

him, but don't get mad at yourself. I'm telling you, you're *not* the one who made it happen."

Brittany sat and ran a thumbnail back and forth across her front teeth, going over in her mind what Julia had said. Julia wasn't like most people. She didn't rush to fill in empty spaces in the conversation. After she finished talking, she just sat there and waited.

"So you don't think it was my fault?" Brittany asked minutes later.

"No, I don't."

Brittany looked up at Julia, and nodded. "Oh."

"You don't believe me, do you?"

"I'm not sure."

Julia went to a shelf, took down a notebook, and handed it to Brittany. "I'm going to ask you to do something—something that I think will help you. I'd like you to begin keeping a journal in this notebook where you can write down your feelings about what happened to you. Will you do that? Then we'll talk about what you've written the next time you come."

"What good will it do to write about what happened?" Brittany asked.

"Why don't you try it and find out for yourself?" She paused. "Someday, Brittany, you'll be on the other side of the mountain. Will you please do this writing exercise? I was going to say, for *me*. But it's really for you. Will you do it?"

"All right," Brittany said.

Julia said it would be a good idea for me to write a journal. She said it would help me get to the other side of the mountain, whatever that means.

I've lost so much. Sometimes when I think about the way I used to be, it's almost like that person is dead. I used to cry at night wishing everything could be the way it used to be—the way it used to be in Idaho with my friends. I was so happy then. I really was. I used to sing in front of people all the time,

155

for talent shows at school and in our ward. I talked to people too. When I walked down the hall in school in Idaho, I was always saying hello to people. I had so many friends then.

Now it's like the person I was is gone. Will I ever be like that again?

I don't sing anymore. It stopped with Derek. Everything stopped with Derek. Sometimes I think the me that used to be died then, too, and all that's left now is an empty shell.

I hate what he did to me. I hate that he pretended to be my friend when all the time he was planning what he was going to do. I hate it that I even agreed to go out with him. I knew he was a little strange, but I really needed a friend at that time. I wonder if I should have used better judgment. But how could I have known what would happen?

I never see Craig anymore. I thought we were friends, but now he never even calls me. Is he afraid I'll corrupt him?

Before Derek hurt me, I used to pray all the time. For every little thing. Like when I had a test coming, or just before I performed. Every night before My Fair Lady I always prayed that I'd do a good job. Back then I felt like God was there for me, that he was always listening to me, and that he loved me. I But after it happened, I quit praying.

I used to call him Father in Heaven, but now I call him God because I can't see how he could be my father and let this happen to me. If he is my Father in Heaven, why didn't he help me when I needed him? I guess I quit praying because I still blame him for what happened. If he has all this power and if he loves me, like people say he does, then why did he let it happen? If I were God, I would never let some jerk like Derek do what he did to me. I'd strike him dead. I would!

I used to like to think of God as this really caring person, but what if he doesn't care all that much about any of us? I'm not saying that's the way it is, but when you've gone through what I went through, it makes you wonder.

There's something else. Something I don't like to talk about.

I don't know how to say this exactly, and I know Julia is going to get mad at me for saying it. I know I'm not broken like a toy or anything like that. It's not physical. I'm not sure how to explain it. It's just that when you grow up in the Church and you've been taught all your life that your first time should be on your wedding night, then when something like this happens, you think everything is lost, and there's nothing you can do about it. And after that, when you go to church, you feel like you're beyond any hope, and there's no reason to even go to church anymore.

I used to think about getting married. I wanted to bring the gift of myself to my marriage. But then Derek robbed me of that by turning it into something vulgar and dirty. That's why I feel so far from Heavenly Father. Derek has made me feel unworthy and unclean. I'm not sure I'll ever feel any different.

Four days later Brittany met with Julia again.

"What are we going to talk about today?" Brittany asked.

"Well, first thing, I see you brought your notebook. Did you write in it?"

"Yes, I did. But it's kind of negative."

"That's okay. May I read it?"

"If you want, but it's not very good."

"I'm sure it will be fine."

Brittany sat and waited while Julia read what she'd written.

When she finished, Julia said, "Well, the thing that encourages me is that you've been able to articulate your feelings. That's good. It gives us a place to begin." She paused. "Today I have something I want you to think about. Ready?"

"I guess so."

"I want you to tell me what it would be like if you truly believed that what happened to you was not your fault, that you were an innocent victim, and that you bear no

157

responsibility or blame for what happened. How would your life be different if you truly believed that?"

Brittany paused. "To tell you the truth, I don't really know."

"Have you ever been waiting in a long line, say for a movie, and had somebody come and cut in line in front of you?"

"Sure, that's happened to me," Brittany said.

"Did you blame yourself that someone cut in front of you?" Julia asked.

"No."

"Really? What if that person were to say to you that he knew you wanted him to cut in line in front of you?"

"I'd tell him he was crazy."

"What if he told you that he could tell from the clothes you were wearing that you wanted him to cut in line in front of you?"

"Same thing."

Julia nodded. "What if he tried to make you feel guilty because he cut in line? What if he claimed you left too much room between you and the person in front of you, and insisted that because you did, it's your fault."

"I know what you're trying to tell me," Brittany said, "but it's not the same."

"Why isn't it the same?" Julia asked. "Did you say to Derek, 'Yes, this is what I want you to do to me'?"

"No, I told him to stop, and I tried to get away."

"So why did he say he knew you wanted it?"

Brittany thought about it a long time. "To make me feel guilty?"

"I think that's right. He wanted you to keep quiet and not tell anyone what happened. But it was not your fault, any-more than it would be your fault if someone cut in line in front of you at the movies. You were a victim. Now, how will your life be different as you totally accept that fact?"

"I don't know."

Julia nodded. "Well, my dear, I think you need to find out."

"Why did it happen to me then?" Brittany asked.

"Some boys are predators. They're like wolves circling a herd of sheep, always looking for a situation they can exploit. I think that Derek was like that. If it wasn't you, it would have been someone else. Every day he went to school, he was looking for opportunities. You need to accept the fact that you don't carry even the slightest responsibility for what Derek did to you. You are totally innocent."

"Then why do I feel guilty? Why do I feel like a bad person?"

"Because you've thought of yourself like that since it happened. It will take time to work this out in your mind. That's why we need to keep seeing each other."

"All my life I've been taught about the importance of chastity. Now when people even mention the word, I feel bad."

"You've been carrying a heavy burden, haven't you?" Julia asked.

"I guess I have. I don't think about it all the time anymore, but I used to. It would be great to go to Young Women's again with a clean conscience."

"You haven't been going?"

"No. I don't feel welcome there."

"Why not?"

"It's hard to put in words. I guess I feel dirty. Are you a Mormon?" Brittany asked.

"Yes, I am."

"Then you should know why I feel guilty."

"I'm sorry, I don't. Could you explain it to me?"

"Because we're told that our first time should be on our wedding night. And it's too late for me to have that happen."

"Brittany, listen to me. Derek did something to you against your will. How does that make you unworthy?"

"Maybe I didn't fight him enough."

"Did you fight him?"

"Yes, but then he pinned me down and started hitting me when I tried to get away, so I quit fighting." She paused. "Also, I didn't scream."

"Why didn't you?"

"Because I thought he'd kill me if I screamed."

"If you told him to stop, if you tried to stop him, then how does that make you responsible for what happened?"

"I don't know, but, don't you see, I've already had my first time. I always thought my first time would be on my wedding night."

"What you experienced has nothing to do with the physical intimacy between a husband and a wife. In all the really important ways, your wedding night will be your first time."

"But it won't be, not really."

"That doesn't mean you can't have a wonderful marriage," Julia said.

"Will my husband be able to tell that it isn't my first time?" Brittany asked.

"Not unless you tell him."

"I thought he would."

Julia got up, walked to the window, and looked out. "You and I can work through some important issues, but there is something else you need to do. There's someone who can give you the help that I can't give."

"Who's that?"

"Your bishop. You need to go to him and tell him what happened."

Brittany shook her head. "I don't think I can do that."

"It will take away much of the guilt you are carrying. He's the one who can help you."

"It would be too embarrassing to tell him."

160

"Is that why you haven't talked to him before now?" Julia asked.

"Yes. I'm afraid that if I were to tell him, he'd call me a child of the devil, or something like that."

Julia smiled sadly. "Oh, Brittany, you're not a child of the devil. Believe me. Nobody is a child of the devil."

"You know what I mean. That he'd tell me I was evil. That he'd get up in sacrament meeting, tell everybody I was a bad person and that everyone should stay away from me."

"Has he ever done that before for anyone in your ward?" Julia asked.

"No."

"Then I doubt if he'd do it in your case. Would you like me to talk to him first before you go in to see him?"

"What would you tell him?" Brittany asked.

"If you give me permission, I'll tell him what happened to you, and how, for a while, you refused to deal with it, but now you're trying to work through it. Also, I'll tell him how pleased I am about the progress you're making."

"Am I making progress?"

"I think you are. Don't you?"

Brittany shrugged her shoulders. "I don't know. Maybe so."

"At least we're talking. That's better than holding it in, isn't it?"

"I guess so."

"What will you say when you tell him what happened to me?" Brittany asked.

"I'll tell him you were the victim of date rape."

Brittany cringed. "I never use that word."

"Why's that?"

"It's not a very nice word."

"It is what happened to you, though, isn't it?"

"Yes."

"It doesn't need to be a dark secret. It would be better if

161

you were able to think of it in the same way you would if you had come down with pneumonia. That's bad too, but it happens sometimes. We don't think poorly about people who get sick, do we? We don't say it was their fault. We don't say they were secretly wanting to get pneumonia. We just say they got it. Maybe you need to think of what happened to you in the same way. Silence protects the perpetrator more than it does the victim. Anyone can be a victim. You can walk out of a store and get robbed in the parking lot. We don't blame people who that happens to, do we? How is what happened to you any different?"

"I don't know."

"I don't know either. Will you go see your bishop if I talk to him first?" Julia asked.

"I guess so."

Brittany gave Julia a hug on her way out. It felt good to have someone on her side.

10

It was seven o'clock on a Sunday night when Brittany sat down in Bishop Holmes' office at his home. His wife and children were in another part of the house, and the house was quiet.

He was a young bishop, a soft-spoken man, who kept his light brown hair short and wore the same charcoal gray suit with a gray striped tie every Sunday. As far as Brittany was concerned, the best thing about him was his wife Shalene, a tall, outgoing, often funny, brunette. Brittany knew their youngest daughter, Celeste, from when Celeste had been in the nursery, before the little girl graduated into Primary.

It was awkward for Brittany to be sitting there, trying to answer the bishop's questions about school and her job when she knew what they were really there to talk about.

After a few minutes of light conversation, it was time to begin.

"Well, Brittany, let me say, first of all, I'm very happy you agreed to come and see me. I hope you feel comfortable talking to me." He leaned forward and rested his elbows on his desk. "I've got all the time in the world. How can I help you tonight?"

"I guess Julia told you why I needed to see you," Brittany

said softly. Her face was flushed, and she could feel her heart pounding.

"Yes, she told me what happened to you. I'm so sorry you had such a horrible experience."

"It was really bad. Do I have to tell you every detail of what happened that night?"

"No, not at all. Only what you feel comfortable in telling me."

She took a deep breath. "Well, okay. Sometimes I worry I didn't fight him enough, I tried to get him to stop, but he was too strong, and every time I tried to get away, he hit me. So, after a while, I quit fighting because I thought he'd kill me if I didn't." She cleared her throat. This was so hard to talk about, but she had to know the answers to her deepest fears. "Was it wrong of me to quit fighting?"

"No. You must have been very frightened. I understand."

She nodded her head, relieved at the answer the bishop had given. "There's something else that's been bothering me. One of the policemen who interviewed me asked me if I screamed. I didn't. But I did keep telling him to stop. The way the policeman asked it, it was like if I didn't actually scream, then I didn't do enough to stop it from happening." She paused. "I've worried a lot about that . . . Nobody ever told me that if this happened to me, I should scream. I didn't know what I was supposed to do."

"Brittany. Let me ask you something. Do you think there was any doubt in the boy's mind whether this was something you wanted to happen?"

"No, he knew I wanted him to stop. I kept saying no and trying to push him away, at least at first, before he started hitting me."

Bishop Holmes wiped a tear from his cheek. In a voice husky with emotion, he said, "You did enough, Brittany."

She was crying now. After a time, she said, "Thank you." She reached for a tissue from the box on the bishop's desk.

"There's one more thing, Bishop. I want to get this all out in the open because if I don't, then I'm afraid some things will keep worrying me. Derek is the name of the boy who did it. Well, when he took me home, he blamed me. He told me that he knew I wanted it."

"Did you?"

"No, I never even thought about things like that."

"Then what he said isn't true, is it?" Bishop Holmes said.

"No, not really. But, for a while I wondered if maybe he was right, that maybe it was partly my fault."

"Julia told me that was one of your concerns, and I agree with her—that he wanted you to believe you were at least partly responsible for what happened. But that's not true. What he did was selfish and evil. You were his victim. You are not in any way responsible, and you must not blame yourself."

"I keep thinking it might have been the way I was dressed. Do you want to know what I was wearing? It was a new pair of jeans, a long sleeved shirt, and a leather vest. What do you think?"

"Are you asking me what clothes could a girl wear that would justify a boy forcing her to have sexual relations with him?"

"I guess I am."

"Nothing justifies date violence, Brittany. He carries full responsibility for what happened—not you—not in the slightest."

"But we're told to dress modestly."

"Were you dressed modestly?"

"Yes."

"I'm sure you were. I've never seen you dress immodestly."

"Thanks." She felt relieved to hear the bishop say that. "This has messed me up so bad. I quit praying and everything. I quit going to Young Women. I've spent a lot of time in the hall during church. This experience has totally changed my personality. I've been afraid of even walking down the halls at school, afraid to be around boys. Sometimes I've had trouble keeping food down. People have told all sorts of bad stories about me. I've never had a lot of friends here, but even the few I've made have turned against me. It's been a nightmare."

"I wish I could have talked to you right after it happened."

"I should've come right away. I can see that now. Part of the reason I didn't though was because I felt really . . . well . . . dirty, I guess. Partly because of knowing things I didn't want to know until I was married. Also, I was so afraid of him. He told me that if I talked to anyone about it, he'd kill me and my mom. So at first I wasn't going to say anything, but then the next day I got to worrying that he might have infected me, like with AIDS. I decided I wanted to go to the hospital and make sure I wouldn't get pregnant or be infected, so I told my mom. I'm so glad I told her. She didn't yell at me or anything. She was angry at Derek and hurt, but I was surprised at how well she handled it. She knew what to do. She got me to the hospital and got me the help I needed, so that was good."

"I'm glad you told her."

"It was hard to tell her. It was hard to come here tonight too. Part of the reason I didn't want to tell you this is because you're so good. I mean, in a way, you're almost too good. To tell you the truth, I didn't even know if you'd understand what the word *rape* means. Or that I'd start to tell you and you'd go running out of the room saying you didn't want to hear such horrible things. I even imagined you'd tell me I was a child of the devil." Brittany smiled. "Julia says I've been watching too many scary movies."

The bishop smiled. "You really thought that's how I'd react?"

166

"Yeah, I kind of did."

"I'm sorry if I've given you that impression. As a bishop, I try to represent the Savior when people come to me like you did tonight. What do you suppose the Savior's reaction would be if you told him what happened to you?"

"I don't know."

"I think he would tell you how sorry he was that this has happened to you."

"Really?"

"Yes, really."

While Brittany tried to imagine what that would be like, the bishop looked up a scripture and then had Brittany read it out loud.

"'Come unto me, all ye that labour and are heavy laden, and I will give you rest. Take my yoke upon you, and learn of me; for I am meek and lowly in heart: and ye shall find rest unto your souls. For my yoke is easy, and my burden is light.'"

The bishop then flipped back to the Old Testament. "This is one of my favorites. 'Cast thy burden upon the Lord, and he shall sustain thee.' How does that make you feel?" he asked.

"Better."

"Good." He reached for his triple combination. "This is in Mosiah, the 18th chapter. 'Now, as ye are desirous to come into the fold of God, and to be called his people, and are willing to bear one another's burdens, that they may be light; Yea, and are willing to mourn with those that mourn; yea, and comfort those that stand in need of comfort, and to stand as witnesses of God at all times and in all things, and in all places that ye may be in, even until death . . .'" He set the book aside and looked over the desk at Brittany. "Please let me teach you how to let the Savior help you with the burden you've been carrying."

Brittany nodded. A sweet feeling of peace washed over

her. She closed her eyes and enjoyed feeling the influence of the Holy Ghost for the first time in a long time. She was crying, but the tears were not bitter. They were soothing.

This was not at all like what Brittany had imagined it would be. She had feared the worst—that the bishop would tell her it was all her fault, or that he'd embarrass her by asking for intimate details of what had happened to her, or that he'd excommunicate her on the spot. But none of those things happened. He seemed to understand how it had been for her. She felt he was on her side, and that he would do anything in his power to help her.

She opened her eyes and looked at the bishop. "You know what? I feel a lot better than I have in a long time."

The bishop nodded. "Can I tell you something? Right now I feel very strongly how much Heavenly Father and the Savior love you."

"Thank you for telling me that." She plucked another tissue from the box on the desk and wiped her eyes.

The bishop leaned forward. "Brittany, can I ask you a question? Do you feel you have lost your chastity because of what happened to you?"

"Yes."

"I don't agree."

Brittany was surprised. "Not even after what he did to me?"

"Not even after that."

"I don't understand. That's what he stole from me."

"No he didn't. Can you recite the Young Women theme?"

"I'm not sure. It's been a while."

"Give it a try, okay?"

She began. "We are daughters of our Heavenly Father who loves us, and we love him. We will 'stand as witnesses of God at all times and in all things, and in all places . . . ' as we strive to live the Young Women Values, which are—Faith,

Divine Nature, Individual Worth, Knowledge, Choice and Accountability, Good Works and Integrity . . . "

"Stop there. Let's talk about choice and accountability. As I understand it, that means we are held accountable for the choices we make. Would you agree with that?"

"Yes."

"Was what happened to you that night a choice you made?"

She shook her head. "No."

"Then you're not held accountable for what happened. We're held accountable only for the choices we make, not for what is imposed on us against our will. Brittany, if you were virtuous before this happened to you, then your virtue is still intact. You can still be married in the temple."

Tears flooded her eyes. "I can?"

"Yes, you can."

It seemed too good to be true. "Are you sure?"

"I'm sure."

"How can you be sure? Don't you have to ask the stake president or someone else, to make sure it's okay?"

"No," the bishop said, smiling, "That's one of the privileges of my calling. I'm the one who makes decisions like that."

"Oh." She had a little cold, so it wasn't just the tears. Her nose was a problem too. She plucked a couple more tissues and blew her nose. She looked for a place to put them, but she couldn't see a waste paper basket, so she set them on the bishop's desk. That didn't look right either. "Sorry," she apologized, "I'm kind of a mess today."

"Looks like you've got the cold that's been going around," he said. "Here, use this," he said, placing his wastebasket where she could get at it.

"Let's see, where were we?" the bishop asked.

"You're sure I can go to the temple some day?"

He smiled. "Brittany, I'm absolutely positive about that."

"That's so hard to believe."

"Why's that?"

"I don't know. I guess I thought I'd lost it all, and that God would never want to have anything to do with me, and there was no hope for me anymore."

"That simply is not true."

"Are you sure?"

He smiled. "I'm sure." He opened a copy of the *For the Strength of Youth* pamphlet and turned to page fifteen. "Would you read out loud where I've underlined, please?"

Brittany began to read. "'Victims of rape, incest, or other sexual abuse are not guilty of sin. If you have been a victim of any of these terrible crimes, be assured that God still loves you! Your bishop can also help and guide you through the mental and emotional healing process if you seek his advice and counsel.'"

"That comes from the First Presidency. Do you suppose you can trust what they say?"

She smiled. "Yes."

"Good."

She sat quietly for a time, then shook her head and said, "I really should have come here sooner. I can see that now."

"I wish you had, but I'm so glad you came today."

Brittany sat with her head lowered, her chin resting on her hand. She could hear the bishop's kids playing. And she could smell either a cake or cookies being baked. "But why did it happen to me?" she asked.

"Good question, and a very natural one to ask. I'm not sure I can answer it in a specific way for your situation, but I think I can answer it in general terms."

"Okay."

"When Heavenly Father put us here on the earth, he provided us with the freedom to make choices. We call that agency. Right?"

"Uh-huh."

The bishop's children were now playing just outside the door. He went to the door and asked them to move and then returned to his desk. "Sorry about that."

"That's okay."

"If you'd rather meet at my office at church, we can do that next time."

"No, I like coming here better."

"It's noisier here than it would be at the church."

"I don't mind the noise."

"You're sure?"

"I am."

"Good. Then we'll continue meeting here. Let's see, where were we?"

"We were talking about us having the freedom to make choices here on the earth."

"Oh yes. Let me ask you a question, Brittany. How do you suppose Heavenly Father felt when they were crucifying the Savior, his Only Begotten Son?"

Brittany turned her gaze downward. "It must have been horrible."

"I'm sure you're right. But he didn't stop it. Why?"

"I don't know."

"Because part of the plan is that we have the freedom to make bad choices without experiencing immediate punishment. If sinful people were instantly punished for their wrongdoing, then, before long, nobody would commit sin. On the surface that doesn't sound too bad, but what freedom would we have then?"

Brittany thought about it. "Not much, I guess."

"That's right. Heavenly Father values agency so much that he didn't even interfere when his own son was being brutalized and murdered. But that doesn't mean that he isn't aware of our suffering and fears."

"But sometimes things aren't fair."

"You're right. That's what the Atonement is all about—to

make things right, either in this life or in the life to come. Let me tell you of a struggle that Joseph Smith himself had about this question."

From outside the closed door, they heard a little girl's voice. "Daddy, do you want a cookie?"

The bishop smiled. "Not now, sweetheart."

"Daddy, we have cookies for you. Mommy made them."

"I'll have one later, Celeste. Right now I'm talking to somebody."

"You're talking to Brittany, Daddy. She's in the nursery."

"That's right. It's Brittany."

"Brittany can have a cookie too. I brought one for her."

"Please excuse me," the bishop said, going to the door.

"I wouldn't mind a cookie," Brittany said with a smile.

The bishop smiled. "Well, me either, actually."

The bishop opened the door and knelt down to take two cookies from his blonde-haired daughter. "Thank you, Celeste. That's really nice of you to think of me and Brittany."

Celeste peeked into the room. "Hi, Brittany!"

"Hi, Celeste. How you doin'?"

"Fine."

The bishop needed his wife to rescue him. "Shalene? Can you please come and get Celeste?"

Sister Holmes came out of the kitchen and whisked Celeste away. "Come on, Celeste. Mommy needs your help."

The bishop closed the door. He put one of the cookies on the desk in front of Brittany and the other on top of his scriptures. "Let's see, where were we?"

"Something about the prophet Joseph Smith."

"Oh yes. Doctrine and Covenants, Section 121. Joseph Smith and several of his friends had been in prison for months. Finally the Prophet couldn't stand it anymore. Out of great frustration, he pleaded with the Lord, 'Let thine anger be kindled against our enemies; and, in the fury of

172

thine heart, with thy sword avenge us of our wrongs.' And what happened?"

"I don't know."

"Let's read it. The Lord said this to Joseph . . . right here . . . if you could read it out loud . . . "

She read from verse seven. "'My son, peace be unto thy soul; thine adversity and thine afflictions shall be but a small moment; And then, if thou endure it well, God shall exalt thee on high; thou shalt triumph over all thy foes.'"

The bishop nodded. "The same thing holds for you, Brittany. If you endure this well, Heavenly Father will exalt you on high, and you shall triumph over all your foes."

"You seem to be sure of that. How come I'm not?"

"It takes time. Just give it time." He paused, then after a moment he asked, "Would you like a priesthood blessing?"

Brittany had not grown up in a home where the priesthood was used. She had envied her friends whose fathers were able to give them blessings, and it struck her as a wonderful thing for the bishop to offer. She would welcome a blessing.

"Yes, please," she said.

"Just a minute. I'll go tell my wife what we're going to do, so we won't be interrupted."

While he was gone, Brittany reached across the desk, grabbed some more tissues, and tried to put herself back together again.

The blessing the bishop gave her was wonderful, not so much for what he said, as for the warm feeling she experienced—that she was loved by Father in Heaven. It was a long blessing, and at times the bishop paused, waiting for the message Heavenly Father was giving him through the Holy Ghost.

By the time it was over, tears had made tiny rivulets down her face and dropped onto her Sunday dress. Her nose was a mess. Afterwards, before she shook the bishop's hand, she grabbed for several tissues so she wouldn't look too awful.

They made an appointment for a week later at the same time.

As she was leaving, Bishop Holmes called her back to give her the cookie Celeste had brought for her.

On the way home, Brittany felt she'd gotten over a huge hurdle in going to see her bishop. Some important things had been clarified for her, and she had experienced a wonderful sense of relief. She was grateful for that. She felt like she had ascended a long way up that mountain that Julia had described.

11

Near the end of July, Brittany got a new job, working at a leather crafts kiosk in the mall. It was a good job for her because she liked working alone. Also, she wasn't busy all the time, and she enjoyed watching people.

One Saturday, Craig dropped by to see her while she was working. He'd been shopping with his mom for his mission clothing. His mom looked tired, and when she saw Craig heading over to talk to Brittany, she told him she'd meet him in the food court. "I really need to sit down," she said.

Craig looked happy. "Hi, stranger. So, you're working here now, right?"

"Yeah. Want to buy something?"

"Probably not. Did you hear I got my mission call?"

"No. Where are you going?"

"Scotland."

"That's great! I'm proud of you."

"I'm so excited."

"When do you enter the MTC?"

"Next week."

"Good for you. You'll be a great missionary."

"I hope so."

"You will."

"It's amazing how much I've had to do to get ready. We've spent so much money today just on suits."

"Yeah, but if you get good quality, they'll last longer."

"Hey, that's what the salesman said," Craig said.

There was an awkward pause. "How's Diana?" she asked.

"She's fine."

"Good."

"Is she going to wait for you?" Brittany asked.

"She says she is."

"I bet she will too."

"We'll see." He paused. "Well, I guess I'd better be going. I'm getting set apart Tuesday night. And then we'll head for the MTC on Wednesday. So this may be the last time I see you for a couple of years."

"Have a good mission."

"Thanks. I'll try." He didn't immediately leave. Instead, he said, "It was great being with you in the play. That was one of the highlights of high school for me."

Brittany felt a rush of emotion. "Thanks. I loved it too." She wished they could talk more, wished they had seen more of each other, but it was too late for that now.

Craig gave her an awkward hug and then waved as he backed away to go find his mother.

There were times when Brittany had felt that Craig had betrayed her by not continuing to be her friend after all the rumors began circulating around school. She always wondered if he believed the things people said about her. She knew she shouldn't blame him for staying away, but she did. She could see how it happened, though. Once she dropped choir, they never saw each other anymore. And then, of course, there was Diana.

It just wasn't meant to be, Brittany thought.

The next Tuesday, right after Brittany got home from work, Diana showed up at her door.

"Can I come in?" she said.

"Yeah, sure."

Brittany was painfully aware of how ordinary their living room was compared to where Diana lived. "Do you want to sit down?"

"Thank you." Diana sat on the edge of the couch, her back straight. She looked like she'd been crying. After a moment, she said, "I came to apologize."

"For what?"

"I've been feeling bad about it ever since it happened, but tonight, I couldn't hide it anymore."

"Tonight?"

"Craig goes into the MTC tomorrow, and he invited me to his setting apart. I just came from his house. The thing is, I knew I couldn't be there for something so sacred if I didn't tell him what I'd done. So I told him. He would've come here himself, but there wasn't time. The stake president needed to set him apart right then. So Craig asked me if I'd come and tell you . . . what I did."

"What did you do?"

"This is really hard. When there were stories going around school about you and Derek, at first Craig didn't believe them. You know what he's like. I knew he'd stand by you, no matter what."

Diana stopped talking, lowered her gaze, and covered her mouth with her hand. "I was afraid . . . " She had to stop to gain control. Shaking her head, she gave it another try. ". . . I was afraid I'd lose him. So I made up lies about you. I told him you had a bad reputation back in Idaho, and that the reason you and your mom moved here was for you to try to get a new start. I told him that if he spent time with

177

you, you might make it so he wouldn't be worthy to serve a mission."

Diana raised her eyes and looked at Brittany. She was struggling to control her emotions. "I can't believe I did that," she said.

Brittany watched her cry but had no compassion. Only anger. "What did I ever do to you to make you want to hurt me so bad?" she demanded.

"Nothing. It was me. I was jealous and afraid. I'm sorry."

Brittany went into the kitchen and got a box of tissues and handed them to her. All she could think of was how much those rumors hurt and how persecuted she had felt at school. "Because of the rumors going around school, I lost all my friends," Brittany said.

"I'm sorry."

"Is that all you can say? Do you *know* what it's like not to have any friends, and to have people whispering about you behind your back? Do you have any idea what that's *like?*"

Diana, her head down and tears streaming down her face, could only shake her head.

Brittany wanted Diana to know the whole story, so she'd know how much damage she'd done. "Do you want to know what really happened to me? Derek date-raped me. That's what happened. And then he made up lies about me. And then you made up more lies about me. So, the way I look at it, you're not much better than him."

Diana stood up. "Please let me try to make it up to you. Let me be your friend."

"My friend! Are you crazy? Why would I want you for a friend? I don't want to ever see you again."

"I'm so sorry."

"Oh, sure. You help put me through the worst experience of my life, then say you're sorry, and I'm supposed to smile and say it's okay. Well, it's *not* okay. And your apology is too little, too late. Thanks for nothing."

Brittany walked to the door and held it open. Without saying anything more, Diana walked out of the house. Trembling with anger and emotion, Brittany watched through the window as she drove away.

A while later the doorbell rang. Brittany's mother answered it, then a short time later knocked on Brittany's bedroom door. "There's someone here to see you."

Wearing one of his new missionary suits, Craig was standing in the living room. His parents were with him.

"Please sit down," Brittany's mother said.

After they were all seated, Craig's father began. "This is a little awkward," he said. "Craig wanted to talk to you, Brittany, but since he's been set apart, the only way he could do that is if we came with him."

Craig cleared his throat and began. "Diana just called me and told me what you said to her . . . about Derek. I didn't know, Brittany. There were all these stories going around about you, and then Diana lied to me about what you were like before you moved here. I just didn't know."

"Why didn't you ask me instead of believing everybody else?"

He shook his head. "I don't know. That's what I should have done."

Craig sat, his shoulders hunched over, his head down. He was obviously embarrassed and ashamed. "I abandoned you when you needed a friend most. I'm sorry." He looked up and into Brittany's eyes. "I will never do that again, not to anyone. I promise."

Brittany stood up. "I accept your apology."

"Can I get you folks anything to drink?" Brittany's mother asked.

Brittany shook her head. "No, Mom. Just let them go. I'm sure they have plenty to do to get ready."

Craig's mother smiled. "Actually, we do."

Craig hung behind after his parents had stepped outside.

He looked like he didn't know what to do. Brittany solved the problem by putting out her hand. "Elder Weston, have a wonderful mission. Good night."

They shook hands briefly and then Brittany stepped back and watched him, once again, walk out of her life.

The next time she met with the bishop, Brittany told him about Diana's visit and her attempt to apologize.

"I hate her for poisoning Craig's mind against me. And, of course, I hate Derek. I'll always hate him for what he did to me."

Bishop Holmes reached for his scriptures.

Brittany could see a sermon coming. "I know what you're going to say, but I can't do what you want me to do," she said before he'd even found the passage he was looking for.

"What do you think I want you to do?"

"Forgive Derek, and forgive Diana. I can't do that. I'm sorry. I just can't."

"It doesn't have to be today. Or even tomorrow. But it's something you should work on. I know it will take some time, and that's all right. When something traumatic happens to us, we have to go through what's called a grieving process. But, in time, as you're prayerful, then perhaps you will be able to forgive those who have treated you so badly." He handed her a passage to read from Doctrine and Covenants 64. "Read verse 10 please."

"'I, the Lord, will forgive whom I will forgive, but of you it is required to forgive all men.'"

Handing the book back, Brittany said, "I don't think I can do that."

"Will you pray about it?"

"Well, I'll pray about it, but I'm not promising I'll ever forgive Derek."

"Eventually we all must learn to forgive those who hurt us."

"Why?"

The bishop thought about it. "One reason is so that we can more fully feel the influence of the Holy Ghost in our lives, but that's not the only reason." He leaned forward in his chair. "Let me ask you something. When you hate someone, how do you feel when you think about them?"

"I don't know. Angry. When I think about Derek, it just makes me crazy. What he did was so mean and selfish, I can hardly stand it."

"Are those pleasant feelings? Do you enjoy being angry and feeling mean?"

"No."

"I know you don't, but the only way to avoid having such feelings is to get rid of the anger. When you are finally able to do that, the anger will go away, and you can experience peace. Does that make sense to you?"

"Well, sure. But I can't do it. Not after what he did to me. You can't expect me to."

"I understand. It isn't easy. But holding on to the anger doesn't hurt anyone but you. Your hating him doesn't create a problem for Derek, but it affects you in a powerful way, doesn't it?"

Bishop Holmes smiled at her. "If you make it a matter of sincere prayer, I know you can eventually find it in your heart to forgive Derek and the others who have offended you. And when you do, the peace you'll experience will be a sweet thing." He paused. "Just give it time."

As Brittany continued to meet with Julia and with her bishop, she began to feel better about herself. Her one regret was agreeing to go out with Derek in the first place. She wished she had said no when he asked her out. The reason she didn't was because she didn't want to hurt his feelings. She wanted to be a nice person. And nice people don't refuse to go out with someone.

181

Even if she had said no, it wouldn't have ended there. Back then she wanted to be everybody's friend and not hurt anybody's feelings. She would have said no, and he would have asked why. She would have made up an excuse why she couldn't go out that night, and he would have asked about the week after. She might have made up another excuse, but eventually after turning him down three or four weeks in a row, she would finally have just given up and agreed to go out with him.

With Julia's help, Brittany decided something important: *I can't have as my first priority to be a nice person,* she thought. *More than anything, I need to be true to myself. I need to be honest, even if it seems to be cruel. If I'm not, then I am setting myself up to be a victim.*

She decided beforehand what she would say if someone she didn't want to date asked her out. She played the scene over and over in her mind.

"You want to go to a movie with me next Friday?"
"No, thanks."
"Why not?"
"I don't like you that much."
"That's cause you don't know me."
"And that's the way I'd like to keep it."
"How come?"
"I don't have to give you reasons, do I? All you need to know is that the answer is no, and it will always be no. But, hey, have a nice day, okay?"

She smiled at the thought of being so totally honest. It felt good to know she could say no and not be talked into going out with a guy she didn't really care for anyway. *Empowered,* Julia would have said.

Though she continued to meet with Bishop Holmes, they had gotten to a point where he asked her to check in with him every Sunday for a few minutes—only to see how she was doing. Her meetings with Julia were ongoing, and Brittany felt she was making progress there.

Some things didn't go away though. She still couldn't walk out to her car alone when she got off work at the mall without feeling some anxiety. It remained difficult to be in a large crowd, and she still panicked when a large boy or man approached her. Even certain smells brought back bad memories—the smell of popcorn, the smell of the brand of hair mousse that Derek had used, or even riding in a car on a rainy night. Any of those things brought back the memory of the terror of that one night.

Even so, she felt the sessions with Julia and her visits with Bishop Holmes were helping.

She still had one big challenge, and that was to finish high school. She would have enough credits to graduate by December. And then she'd never have to go to that school again.

12

"Brittany, you know our youth are scheduled to go to the temple to do baptisms for the dead next week, don't you?" Bishop Holmes asked in one of their Sunday sessions near the middle of August.

"Yeah, I know that."

"I noticed you didn't sign up when they passed the list around in Young Women. Is that right? How come?"

"I'm not sure if I should even be in the temple," she said.

"Why do you say that?"

"You know. I'm not exactly the same as the other girls."

"Is it all right with you if I interview you to go to the temple to do baptisms for the dead? Just to see where you stand?"

"I guess."

She was surprised. With each question, she felt more encouraged. And when it was over, the bishop said, "You're worthy to enter the temple to do baptisms for the dead."

"Are you sure?"

"I'm sure. Please go to the temple with us, Brittany."

Brittany didn't say much on the way to the temple, but nobody noticed because the bishop's van was full of youth from the ward. They parked the van in the temple parking lot and walked toward the temple. Brittany hung behind the others. She wanted to savor this moment. It would be her first time in the temple.

The bishop presented the group recommend form to a temple worker. Names were checked off one by one until they were all inside the temple. And then they were issued baptismal clothes and instructed to put them on. After they were all dressed, the group was asked to wait in a room located across from the baptismal area. A large, plate glass window at the front of the room provided an unobstructed view of the beautiful font.

While they were waiting, Bishop Holmes spent a few minutes talking to them.

"The work you'll be doing here today will have eternal consequences. Each name represents a person who lived and died without a knowledge of the restored gospel. I want to read something to you. This happened in the Logan Temple.

"*Probably one of the mightiest preachers the Mormon church ever had was Apostle Melvin J. Ballard. He had had Heavenly manifestations, and did not hesitate to declare the word of the Lord, and with power.*

"*Elder Ballard sat at our baptismal font one Saturday while nearly a thousand baptisms were performed for the dead. As he sat there, he contemplated on how great the temple ordinances were, and how we are bringing special blessings to the living and the dead. His thoughts turned to the spirit world, and he wondered if the people there would accept the work we were doing.*

"*Elder Ballard said: "All at once a vision opened to me, and I beheld a great congregation of people gathered in the east end of the font room. One by one, as each name was baptized for, one of these people climbed a stairway over the font to the west end of the room. Not one soul was missing, but*

185

there was a person for every one of the thousand names bap-
tized that day.

"Brother Ballard said that he had never seen such happy
people in all his life, and the whole congregation rejoiced at
what was being done for them.

"For the rest of his life, Apostle Ballard preached to the
Church in all his travels, that the work we do in the temples
is accepted, and that the people themselves are permitted to
attend and receive the blessings personally.'"

Bishop Holmes's voice got a little husky as he finished
reading the account. "I want you to know," he said, "that the
work you will do here today is vitally important to those
who are waiting for these ordinances. I can imagine that
someday they will thank you for doing something for them
they could not do for themselves. It is a wonderful thing to
serve in the temple, and I am grateful to be here with you."

Brittany felt that the bishop was speaking directly to her
when he concluded by saying, "You will eternally bless those
individuals you will be baptized for today. And, in doing this,
your life will also be blessed."

The work began. While waiting for their turn, Brittany
and the others watched through the window as others were
being baptized for the dead. Each youth entered the font and
was baptized ten times.

I'm in the temple, Brittany thought. *I didn't think this*
would ever happen.

She looked down at her white baptismal clothes. They
were clean and smelled fresh, and she felt clean.

She decided to pray. She didn't say any words. She didn't
even close her eyes. She didn't want anyone to know she
was praying.

Father in Heaven, she thought, *I'm here in your temple.*
The bishop said it would be all right for me to come. I hope it
is.

Tears started to roll down her cheeks. *I feel so good being*

here. All my life I've dreamed about going to the temple some-
day. And now I'm here. Not to be endowed and not to get
married, but I'm here, and it feels so good. It's so quiet and
peaceful, and being here makes me feel like I'm an okay per-
son. I don't feel guilty anymore. After what happened, I didn't
know if you could love me anymore. I felt like I'd let you
down. I wasn't sure if you'd even listen to my prayers. Right
now, though, I don't feel that way. I feel that you're listening
to this prayer and that you love me.

Brittany blinked back her tears.

Father in Heaven, I'm sorry that I blamed you for what
happened. It wasn't your fault. I know that now. And it
wasn't your will that it happened. I was set up by Derek and
his friends. They planned it way in advance. If it hadn't been
me, it would've been some other girl. Maybe some girl who
wouldn't get help like I've done. Maybe she wouldn't tell any-
body and just try to keep the pain inside her. I know now, that
isn't the right thing to do. Sometimes I think about that other
girl, like I took her place, like maybe I helped her so she
wouldn't have to go through what I have. Then there would
be some good come from my experience.

That's what I want, that some good will come from this,
that my experience will help other girls in some way, either so
it doesn't happen to them, or else that they will get the help
they need so they can get through it, then move on with their
life.

Brittany interrupted her prayer, sitting quietly with her
eyes now closed. She felt at peace and totally comfortable.
She thought about what she was about to do and continued
her silent prayer.

I'm going to be baptized today for women who died with-
out knowing about the restoration of the gospel. I wish I could
see them like Elder Ballard did. I'm not really asking for that,
but it would be nice if I could at least feel something.

I'll be baptized ten times today. Are these ten women

excited about this? I hope so, because I am. I hope what the bishop said is true, that someday, after I die, I'll be able to meet them. I want them to know that this is my gift to them. Please tell them I have love in my heart for them today.

She paused again, thinking about where she was. *Father in Heaven, I just want you to know how happy I am to be in your temple. I feel like it's all right with you that I'm here. I love you now more than ever before. And I know that you love me too.*

She concluded her prayer: *Just one more thing. Sometimes the memory of what happened to me comes over me like a dark cloud. When that happens, it's like I can't breathe, and it takes away my hope. Please help me. I know I'll never forget what happened to me, but if you could take away my worry that I did something wrong, that would help so much.*

A few minutes later they called her name, and she entered the baptismal area. There was a girl ahead of her being baptized, and the temple worker signaled for Brittany to sit down on a bench until it was her turn.

The girl in the font was just a Beehive. Every time she came out of the water, she wiped her hair out of her eyes, just in time to be submerged once again in the water. Brittany had to smile because of the girl's futile attempt to be presentable.

"That's all," the recorder said. "Next, please."

The Beehive came out of the font and was handed a towel, and Brittany stepped to the font. As she descended into the water, she glanced up and saw Bishop Holmes standing across the way, behind the glass window, watching her.

He smiled and nodded his head, and Brittany gave him probably the biggest grin he'd ever seen from her. *I'm ready now. I'm so ready,* she thought as she took her position in the font.

Brittany listened carefully to each name, and each time she was immersed, she repeated the woman's name in her mind and thought, *I'm doing this for you.*

When Brittany walked into the house that night, her mother asked her how it had gone. Instead of immediately answering, she gave her mother a long hug. Finally, she said, "I feel so good. This is why you work at the temple every week, isn't it? Because of the way you feel while you're there."

"Yes, that's why."

They sat at the kitchen table and had cookies and milk and talked until after eleven o'clock. And then they had family prayer together, just the two of them.

It had been a long time since Brittany felt as peaceful and happy as she felt that night.

By the end of August, business at the leather-crafts booth was down quite a bit. Most of their orders came near Christmas. That meant Brittany had a lot of time with nothing to do. She didn't mind though. She enjoyed watching people in the mall. But one day she saw something that at first alarmed her and then made her angry.

It was nothing dramatic. Two girls were hanging out at the mall after school. They looked to be about twelve or thirteen years old.

Two boys watched them walk by. The boys were older, maybe fifteen. They were both wearing jeans, which hung so low on their hips Brittany wondered how they kept them from falling down.

When the two young girls walked past them, one of the boys said something, and the girls stopped to talk. From where she was, Brittany couldn't hear what was being said, but she didn't like the looks of what was going on.

Walk away, Brittany thought. *Those guys are losers.*

After a time, the four kids walked off as two couples.

That's a mistake, Brittany thought.

An hour or so later the four walked by her kiosk again. By now, one of the boys had his arm draped around the taller girl's waist, and the two couples stopped to lean on a railing and listen to a mariachi band playing on a lower level. They were about twenty-five feet from Brittany, and she watched them.

The boy with the taller girl kept massaging the girl's back. And then he pulled her close and whispered in her ear. She hunched her shoulders and pulled away, but she was laughing.

Brittany felt sick. She knew these boys were trouble and was equally certain that the girls had no clue what was going on. *If they had any idea what could happen, they would run away,* she thought. But eager for the attention, the girls stayed around, even though the taller girl looked as though she was uncomfortable having the boy paw her back and shoulders. From time to time, she would brush his hand away. *Maybe she thinks she can handle this,* Brittany thought. *Big mistake.*

When the boy slid his hand under the girl's jacket and began to rub her back, Brittany couldn't stand it any longer. She left her booth and walked over to where the couples were standing.

"Excuse me," she said.

The taller girl looked irritated. "What?"

"This guy is no good for you."

"Who are you?" the boy asked.

Brittany ignored the boy and looked at the girl. "Don't leave the mall with him. Call your folks and have them come and get you."

"Let's go," the boy said. "We don't have to listen to this."

They left, and Brittany watched them go.

She never saw them again. She had no idea what happened, but she couldn't sleep that night. She kept thinking about the two girls—not only them, but all the girls like them who mistake attention for genuine affection.

Before she went to bed, she knelt by her bed and prayed for those two girls—that what had happened to her would not happen to them.

Two days later the executive secretary in the ward called Brittany to say the bishop wanted to speak to Brittany on Saturday, before or after she went to work. Brittany was confused because she usually saw him on Sundays, after church.

"Are you sure he said Saturday?" she asked.

"Yes, I'm sure."

"Well, okay, but ask him if that's what he really meant."

"I'll call you back if there's any change."

On Saturday morning, Brittany met with the bishop in his office at home. He got right to the point.

"Brittany, The Lord is calling you to be the Laurel class president."

Brittany was stunned. "Bishop, are you certain that Heavenly Father wants me?"

Bishop Holmes smiled. "No mistake. That's what he wants."

Even a few months before, she would not have been able to accept such a call, but after a moment's thought, she said, "I'll do it then."

After she left the bishop, as she was driving home, Brittany whispered a prayer. "Heavenly Father, you told the bishop, but I need to know. Please tell me if this is what you want me to do."

At first she felt nothing, but after a moment, a comforting assurance—a sweet peace—washed over her. She had felt it before and knew what it meant. Heavenly Father loved her. He had always loved her.

The next day, when the Laurels were asked to sustain her, she was tempted to look around to see if any of them had a shocked look on her face, but she didn't. At least none of them gasped.

Two weeks later, Brittany was conducting the opening exercises of the Young Women meeting. She found herself looking at the twelve-year-old girls. One of them had graduated from Primary just a week before and this was her first time to attend Young Women. Brittany remembered the two girls at the mall who were being hit on by the two older boys, and she felt a strong desire to talk to the younger girls about what had happened to her. She dismissed the feeling at first because she knew it would be embarrassing, and she wasn't sure if she would be able to open herself up enough to tell her story. But the impression wouldn't go away. *If I could help even just one of these girls, it would be worth it,* she thought.

She didn't feel comfortable yet talking to her Laurel class adviser or the Young Women president about the idea. But she did feel close enough to the bishop to talk to him. She cornered him after church and told him about her idea.

"I think it could be worthwhile, but I have some concerns," he said.

"Like what?"

He glanced at his scriptures on the desk, reached for his triple combination, and slowly turned to a passage. "This is what Jacob said to his people. 'And also it grieveth me that I must use so much boldness of speech concerning you, before your wives and your children, many of whose feelings are exceedingly tender and chaste and delicate before God, which thing is pleasing unto God . . . '"

He stopped reading. "My niece is in the ward. She just turned twelve. She's a wonderful girl. I don't think she's ever had a bad thought come into her mind, and I'm not sure I want her to know how depraved some people can be."

"I know," Brittany said, and then added. "I was just like her once."

The bishop pursed his lips. "I know you were." He nodded his head. "Go ahead with what you had in mind, but I would like to see an outline of what you intend to present."

It was a month later, on a fast Sunday, when Brittany spoke in a special fireside held for all the young women in her ward. Without naming names and skipping the details of what Derek had done to her, Brittany told the group what had happened to her. She didn't dwell on that but moved quickly to talk about what followed, especially what she had learned from meeting with Julia and with the bishop. She talked about the importance of not keeping something like that hidden and not blaming yourself. She said it is important to tell a parent and to get immediate medical attention, as well as notify the police and identify the abuser. She admitted that it didn't seem like Derek got much of a punishment, and told how she was still struggling to forgive him.

She talked about how hard it was for her to be the subject of rumors and lies and how painful it was to have her friends turn away from her. She also described Julia's involvement and how important it was to get into counseling. She told the girls how angry she had been and described how the bishop had helped her deal with that and get over her guilty feelings.

She explained to the girls how if you are a victim, you can't just pretend it never happened. You have to get help in order to heal—both psychologically and spiritually.

Brittany had written out her talk for the bishop to look at, but she found she didn't need to look at her paper. It was something she had lived through, it was part of her life, and for almost an hour she shared her experience and described what she had learned.

Brittany concluded by bearing her testimony: "I know that Heavenly Father loves me, that he has always loved me, and that what happened to me was not his will. I know that now. I know that every blessing that can come to a person is still available to me, even after what happened to me. I know that. I just have to do the best I can."

She opened her Bible. "This has really been helpful to me. It is from the Bible Dictionary and is the definition of *grace*."

She began to read: "'It is through the grace of the Lord Jesus, made possible by his atoning sacrifice, that mankind will be raised in immortality, every person receiving his body from the grave in a condition of everlasting life. It is likewise through the grace of the Lord that individuals, through faith in the atonement of Jesus Christ and repentance of their sins, receive strength and assistance to do good works that they otherwise would not be able to maintain if left to their own means. This grace is an enabling power that allows men and women to lay hold on eternal life and exaltation after they have expended their own best efforts.'"

With tears in her eyes, Brittany said, "All we have to do is do the best we can."

The room was silent.

"Are there any questions?" she asked.

None of the girls even looked up.

"I have a question," the Young Women president said. "How can what happened to you be avoided?"

Brittany nodded, reached into her pocket and pulled out the wallet-sized version of *For the Strength of Youth*. "I think we all need to read these suggestions at least once a month. The important thing is to always be involved in group activities with people we know. If we do that, I think that will go a long way toward keeping us out of danger."

"Anything else?" the Young Women president said.

"I did some reading to prepare for this talk. One thing I found out is that most of the time things like this happen in somebody's home when there is nobody else around. So I think girls should never go into a home alone with a boy. I know I never will, no matter how much I trust the boy." She paused. "There's one other thing. If you're ever in a situation where you just don't feel right, then trust that feeling and get out of there."

They were out of time. They sang one verse of "I Need Thee Every Hour," had a prayer, and it was over.

Brittany wasn't sure if it had done any good, but at least she had tried.

Being the Laurel class president made one change in Brittany's plans. She made some good friends and enjoyed the experience so much she decided against finishing high school in December. Instead, she decided to take a few more classes and graduate with her class at the regular time at the end of May.

In February Mr. Andrews, the drama teacher, invited Brittany to perform in another school musical.

"Oh no, I don't think so. Thanks anyway."

"Please, we need you badly."

"I'm way out of practice. I haven't sung since the closing night of *My Fair Lady*."

"That is such a waste. Please, at least consider it."

"What play are you doing?" Brittany asked.

"*The Music Man*. Here's the video of the movie version. I'd like you to watch it before you decide."

"I don't think so."

Mr. Andrews was persistent. "I had you in mind to play the part of Marian. She's the female lead."

"I don't even know if I can sing anymore."

He forced the video into her hand. "Just watch this, okay?"

She watched it that night. The charm of the music and the happy ending made it tempting. She kept imagining herself playing the part of Marian. It would be a lot of work, but it would be fun.

The next morning she told Mr. Andrews she'd do it.

Once again, life was good.

13

Being in *The Music Man* that spring was the highlight of Brittany's senior year. Because she was a senior, and an excellent singer, many in the cast looked up to her. The boy playing the male lead was only a junior, and didn't have as much experience onstage, so Brittany worked with him. They became friends, but there was never any possibility of a romance developing between them.

Andrea also tried out for the part of Marian. When she didn't get it, and found out that Brittany had, she refused to be in the play. When someone asked Brittany about it, she shrugged and said, "That's her choice."

With Derek and his friends dropped out of school and gone, it was almost as if the high school had cleansed itself. Brittany had seen him a couple of times during the early part of the school year, but then she heard that he had moved to Alaska, which was a relief. At least there was no danger of running into him.

The three nights of *The Music Man* were fun for Brittany, but she was spared both the highs and the lows that had been a part of her involvement with *My Fair Lady*. At the cast party, following the last performance, Brittany watched the video of the play then went home.

That April Craig began writing Brittany. At first she wasn't sure why, but then, in one of his letters, he told her that Diana was engaged to someone she'd met at BYU.

Brittany didn't place any significance to the fact they were writing. By now she thought of Craig as only a friend. His letters were short and revealed his zeal for what he was doing. For her part, she wrote newsy and encouraging letters.

She applied to both Ricks and BYU but was not accepted at either school. She knew it was because her grades had suffered in her junior year, during the time she was struggling in the aftermath of what Derek had done to her. Once again she felt bitter. Though she had made a lot of progress, there was part of her that was resigned to the idea that she'd never fully recover from what had happened to her, that she'd go the rest of her life being made to suffer again and again.

Thanks, Derek, now I can't even get into the college I want.

She knew she couldn't handle this by herself. She went to see Julia once again.

Julia listened to her for a long time without making any suggestions.

"Don't you have any advice?" Brittany asked.

"Yes, I do."

"What is it?"

"Don't give up your dream. If you could have your choice of Ricks or BYU, which one would you pick?"

"Ricks. They have a good music program. Besides, I need to get away from Utah for a while."

"Then try them again."

"They've already turned me down."

"Call and talk to them. Find out if there's any way you can get in."

"It won't do any good."

Julia handed Brittany the phone. "I'm surprised at you. If you've learned anything, it should be to never give up."

She felt helpless. "I don't know the number."

"Brittany?" Julia said with raised eyebrows.

"All right, all right."

A few minutes later a woman in admissions was giving her the bad news. "I'm sorry. We have already turned down over two thousand students for fall semester this year."

"I see. Well, thank you very much." Brittany reached to hang up.

Julia grabbed the phone. "Hello? My name is Julia Gardner. I'm a counselor at a crisis center for children and youth. I've been working with Brittany for some time now. A year ago she was the victim of date rape. It was not until much later she began to receive counseling. As you might imagine, her grades suffered. If you'll look at her transcript before then, I think you'll find that she was an outstanding student. I'm convinced she has recovered sufficiently to succeed now . . . Yes, I understand you've finished the selection process . . . I see. Well, what would you suggest if she were *your* daughter?"

Julia listened for some time, cradling the phone between her shoulder and ear. She made some notes on her pad. Finally, she said, "Thank you very much. I appreciate your help. Good-bye."

She hung up.

"What did you find out?" Brittany asked.

"Ricks isn't very full in the summer. Why don't you plan on starting second summer term? The person I was talking to said she thinks that if I write a letter explaining your situation, that they may let you in for one of their summer terms."

"And then what?"

"If you do well, they'll let you stay."

"So maybe I can go to Ricks after all?"

"I think so."

Brittany sat there fighting back the tears. "I don't know what I'd do without you."

"I didn't do anything."

Brittany thought about leaving home and about not having access to Julia. She took a deep breath. "Wow. That'd be a big step. I wonder how I'll handle it—you know, being on my own."

"You'll do fine. Just fine."

"I can't believe this is really happening!" Brittany exclaimed as she and her mother drove to Rexburg for the second summer session. The car was packed so tightly that it was practically impossible to see anything out the rear view mirror. For that reason her mother didn't trust herself to change lanes. Much to Brittany's frustration, they stayed in the right lane most of the time.

"I don't suppose we could take a side trip, could we?" she asked her mother as they neared the turnoff that would take them to Grace.

Her mother shook her head. "Better not. It'd take too much time. I have to be at work in the morning."

"It's okay. I'll make it down there some other time."

Other than stopping once for gas, and occasionally at a rest stop to use the restroom, they stayed on the move. To save money, Brittany's mother had packed a lunch, which they ate on the road, during a stretch when Brittany was driving.

"I forgot to ask about an ironing board," her mother said. "Do you know if there's an ironing board where you'll be living?"

"I don't, Mom."

"I should have thought of that. It would be a shame to

have to buy one, especially if it's just for you. If you need to buy one, maybe you and your roommates could go in together on it."

"Sure, Mom, that's a good idea." Realizing they were going to be separated, Brittany felt a sudden sadness.

"I could send one up," her mother continued, "but the shipping might cost as much as getting a cheap one."

How will I make it without my mom, she thought. *She's done so much for me. I'll never be able to repay her for what she's done.*

"We'll ask when we get there."

"Sure, Mom." She dabbed at her eyes.

"Are you okay?"

"I'm okay." But she wasn't. Tears were making it hard to drive. She pulled over to the side of the road and stopped the car.

"We aren't supposed to stop here," her mother said.

"I know."

"What is it?"

Through tears, she blurted out. "Mom, I've never thanked you for all you've done for me. I don't think I could have made it without you. You helped me so much. I just want to thank you for always being there for me."

Her mother started to tear up too, but, even so, she turned back to see what cars were coming to make sure they'd be safe there.

"I love you so much, Mom."

"Oh, Brittany, I love you too, my darling girl." They started laughing through their tears because they had to reach across two boxes to get close enough to hug.

When they arrived in Rexburg, they found there was an ironing board in the apartment after all.

On her first Sunday, Brittany met Rhett Samuelson at church. He was also a freshman, from Logan, Utah, and like

Brittany, his grades were marginal enough that he had been accepted only if he attended a summer session.

Rhett was outrageously handsome, with copper-toned red hair, blue eyes, and a rich, deep voice that made everything he said sound terribly important. But even more wonderful than all that, Rhett had his own car. When he mentioned to Brittany that he was going home to Logan the next weekend, she asked if he'd be willing to drop her off in Grace. "It's practically on your way."

When Rhett said he would, Brittany called Mindy Aldridge, but she wasn't home. Brittany talked to Mindy's mother instead and made arrangements for a weekend visit.

On Friday, the drive gave Brittany and Rhett a good opportunity to talk. Rhett was planning to finish his freshman year and then leave on his mission. He had a wonderful singing voice and, like Brittany, had done some performing in high school. He was planning to major in Theatre Arts.

The closer they got to her old hometown, the more excited Brittany became. As they drove through town a short time later, Brittany couldn't help feeling Grace was smaller than she remembered it. "Turn right just up there," she said.

"Okay. Who are you going to see?"

"Mindy Aldridge. She was my best friend all the way through school until we moved to Utah. It's that house."

Rhett stopped in front of a small, white, one-story farmhouse.

"Would you mind waiting for a minute? I'd like you to meet Mindy."

As Brittany approached the house, it felt as if she'd never left. She knocked on the door because although there was a bell, it had never worked.

Mindy came to the door. "Oh, my gosh! Brittany!" she squealed. They threw their arms around each other. "I can't believe it!"

The two girls sat down together at the same old, round

oak dining table they'd grown up around, jabbering about old times and filling each other in on their lives.

"You look so good," Brittany said. And it was true. Mindy had grown a few inches. Her figure had filled out, and she'd gotten rid of her glasses, changed to contact lenses, and become more sure of herself.

They were both disappointed when they realized that while Brittany would be attending Ricks in the fall, Mindy would be going to ISU in Pocatello. "We never get this right, do we?" Mindy said. "Oh, by the way, how did you get here?"

"Oh, my gosh! I forgot about Rhett! He drove me down. He's been in the car all this time."

"Rhett? Who's he? Tell me all about him," Mindy said with a teasing grin. She still had her crop of freckles, and when she smiled, she wrinkled up her nose the way she always had.

"He's just a guy I met last week."

"Yeah, right," Mindy scoffed. "Is this anything serious?"

"No, not at all. We're just friends."

"Is he hot?"

"Hot? I don't know. He's just a guy."

"Bring him in. I'll tell you if he's hot or not."

Brittany ran out to the car. "Rhett! I am *so* sorry to leave you out here like this. We just started talking, and I lost track of time."

"It's okay, no problem."

"Come on in. I want you to meet Mindy."

Inside the house, Mindy took one look at Rhett and suddenly became tongue-tied.

The three of them stood a little awkwardly together in the doorway. Mindy practiced being speechless and stared at Rhett while Brittany explained that he was on his way home to Logan.

He had carried Brittany's canvas bag into the house from

the car. "Do you want me to take this home with me? Or will you be needing it here?" he teased, flashing one of his handsome smiles.

He handed the bag to Brittany, then said, "Well, I better get going. Nice to meet you, Mindy." He gave a little salute. "Ladies," he said, backing out of the front door.

"Thanks for the ride, Rhett," Brittany called after him.

He hesitated before getting in the car and asked, "Will you need a ride back on Sunday night? I could stop on my way."

"Do you mind?"

"I'm at your service," he said, bestowing another of his killer smiles on them. "How about nine o'clock or so?"

"He is definitely *hot!*" Mindy said as he drove away.

"Well, the stone woman speaks," Brittany teased.

"I think I was struck dumb," Mindy laughed.

"You want me to line you up with him?"

"Would you? I mean, what about the two of you?"

"No problem. Like I told you, we're just friends."

Brittany hardly noticed what they ate for supper. She and Mindy ate in the backyard, sitting at the family's weathered picnic table, not far from a rope swing hanging from a tall cottonwood tree. The two of them had practically grown up playing on that swing.

While they were eating dessert, Mindy asked, "You want to walk through the school for old-times sake?"

"Sure, but it'll be closed now, won't it?"

"Yeah, but Uncle Howard is still the superintendent of schools. I'm sure we can get in."

Fifteen minutes later Mindy's uncle unlocked the door of the old school and let them in. He was a kindly man, but he didn't understand why his niece and Brittany would need to walk through the building at night.

"I'll lock it back up. When you're done, just close the door," he said. "How long will you be?"

"Not long," Mindy said.

The high school and the junior high had been built next to each other, sometime in the fifties. Over the years the girls had attended both, and everything was familiar.

There was plenty of sunlight left in the day, so they didn't need to turn on the lights. They went first to the school's most distinctive furnishing, something few schools could match—an eight-foot-tall stuffed grizzly bear. Its ferocious figure was enclosed in glass and mounted on wheels so it could be moved around.

Brittany and Mindy then strolled through both floors of the two-story school, recalling the times they had spent there. Every room and almost every locker and drinking fountain brought back memories.

After walking the hallways, they ended up in the gym. A dull red light from the sunset shone through the dusty windows. They sat down on an old rolled-up tumbling mat to talk.

"I missed having a friend like you after I moved," Brittany said.

"I'm sure you made plenty of friends," Mindy replied with her usual upbeat optimism.

"No, I didn't, not anyone like you, not someone I could really talk to." Her voice grew softer. "The truth is . . . I had a hard time after I moved." She paused. "Something really bad happened, Mindy."

"What?"

Brittany knew what to say and how to say it. She'd told her story before—to her mother, to Julia, to the girls in Young Women, but relating it to Mindy was very hard. Through her ordeal, she'd kept the memory of this school and her friends in Grace tucked away in her mind, like items in a shrine. She had often recalled the sounds of sprinkler systems going night and day, the crunching of snow at recess, the laughter and fun she and Mindy had shared. Her memories of this place were the only part of her life that Derek had not contaminated. And now she was bringing him and what he had done to her back to this town.

She took a deep breath and began. "Not long after we moved to Utah, I was a victim of date rape."

Mindy's mouth dropped open. "Oh, my gosh! How awful!"

They talked in muted tones, sitting close together, their heads touching, brushing away their tears.

After Brittany finished telling her story, Mindy said, "I know some girls here who have gone through the same thing."

"In Grace?" Brittany asked.

"Yes. Does that surprise you?"

Brittany was stunned. "It does. I never imagined something like that happening here."

"It probably happens everywhere."

"I suppose. It's just that I've thought of this as a sheltered, innocent place. That blows me away."

By the time they'd finished talking, the room was dark except for the exit light, but it provided enough light for them to make it across the wooden gym floor to the hall.

"When are you coming down again?" Mindy asked as they were walking home.

"I don't know."

"Make it soon," Mindy said. Then with a sly grin, she added, "Maybe next time Rhett can stay a little longer. I'm telling you, Brittany, he is *so* hot!"

Brittany started laughing. She felt good again. Everything was familiar. Everything was the way it was supposed to be.

She'd come home.

14

For Brittany, the highlight of her freshman year at Ricks was getting to know her roommates and the boys in her family home evening group. That, and feeling safe most of the time, were the best parts. The negative was never having enough time. On top of classes and homework, she worked part of every day for the college food service, making the sandwiches that were stocked in vending machines around campus.

Brittany, Rhett, and his roommates became good friends. They didn't really date. Mostly they just hung out together. And once or twice a month, Rhett, Brittany, and Mindy would do something. Sometimes Rhett would provide another guy for Brittany, but most of the time she was content to be part of their threesome.

It was much better for Brittany to spend time with freshmen boys because they still had missions to serve, and there was no pressure to get serious. She went out a few times with returned missionaries, but never encouraged them. She didn't want to get caught in any kind of relationship with anyone.

"Once they come home knowing the commitment pattern, watch out," she once told a roommate.

Her advice didn't have much effect on two of her roommates, who each ended up getting engaged by the end of fall semester. Brittany was happy for them, but relieved it wasn't her. She wasn't ready for that.

Because money was tight, Brittany needed to get through Ricks as fast as possible. She decided to attend school during the summer again the next year, so she could be done by the end of fall semester.

Brittany was in her third summer session when Craig returned home from his mission. Without a car and very little money, she wasn't able to get to Salt Lake for his homecoming. Besides, she wasn't sure she wanted to open up that chapter of her life again. But she did call Sunday night and talk to him. He sounded good but a little bewildered, almost depressed, about leaving his mission.

When he asked her when she'd be coming home again, she said she didn't know.

"I'll come up and see you then," he said.

"It's four hours up and four hours back."

"I don't care. I'll come as soon as I can."

After she hung up, she wondered if she sounded like she didn't care whether she saw him or not. Actually, she didn't know her own mind and wasn't sure how she felt. But she finally decided she did want to see him. At least once.

On Friday night, he showed up at her door. "Hi there," he said.

"Hello," she said, a little surprised he'd actually come.

At first it was kind of unreal, seeing each other. She was nervous, and she could see that he was also. They both struggled a bit to know what to say to each other.

He still had the mischievous smile of a little boy. She had always loved his smile, but now there was something more behind it—a kind of warmth that had not been there before. And his eyes. From the times when he had first gazed into her eyes during the play rehearsals, she had always been captivated by them. The eyes hadn't changed.

As he stood in the doorway of her apartment, she noticed he had the beginning of what might end up being a receding hairline. The way he combed his hair made it evident he was self-conscious about it. She didn't mind it though. In some ways it made him more like everybody else, with a few flaws they wished they didn't have.

"You look good, Craig."

"You too. Aren't you going to ask me in?" he asked.

"Yes, of course, come in."

He stepped inside, introduced himself to her roommates, and talked to them. Brittany stood there, watching him with interest. He was different. The same, but different. He didn't have the kind of cockiness he'd displayed in high school. More *genuine*. That's the word that came to her mind.

After they had gone for ice cream and spent some time visiting, he said, "I was wondering if you'd like to go on a hike with me tomorrow."

"Sure, I guess so."

"I thought we could climb in the Tetons. What if we leave here about nine in the morning? We should be back about nine that night."

"All right. Would you like me to pack a lunch?"

"That'd be great. We can eat supper in Jackson on our way home. Well, I've got to run. I'll be spending the night with my uncle and aunt in Mud Lake. So I'll see you in the morning."

As she watched him leave, she thought to herself, *He'll be here tomorrow, we'll go for a hike, and then he'll go back home. And that will be that. We don't need to talk about what happened to me. We're just friends, anyway. That's all we've ever been.*

The next morning they drove to Jenny Lake Lodge, parked, took a boat across the lake, and began hiking. At first the trail was full of other hikers, and they had someone take their picture in front of Hidden Falls and then moved on to Inspiration Point. They had one more picture taken there before continuing upward. As they hiked, the number of people on the trail thinned out, and they enjoyed talking.

She encouraged him to talk about his mission, and he was anxious to do so. What struck her most was the love he expressed for the people of Scotland.

Their hike took them into the most magnificent scenery she'd ever seen. They walked until they were on the back side of the Grand Teton and could see the same view as the one from Rexburg on a clear day. If they continued on the trail they were on, they could have walked back into Idaho.

Around two in the afternoon, they stopped for lunch. They ate sitting by the side of a creek and soaking their feet in the ice cold water for as long as they could stand it. Afterward, they dried on a sweatshirt and laughed about how numb their feet were. Brittany was surprised how at ease she felt with Craig. Being with him was very comfortable for her.

The last boat was scheduled to leave the dock at six P.M. If they missed it, they would have to walk another three miles to get back to the car. Craig looked at his watch. "We'd better start back."

"Okay."

On the way back, they sang snippets of songs from *My Fair Lady*.

"We still sound good together, don't we?" she said.

"I know. Amazing, isn't it? Being in *My Fair Lady* is still one of my best memories from high school. How about you?"

"It was a lot of fun, wasn't it?" She tried to be upbeat but she couldn't help but remember Derek coming backstage after opening night and thrusting a rose in her hand. She had

209

come to view the rose as just another weapon in his arsenal of deceit.

"We were doing so good together for a while," Craig said.

"During the play, sure," she said.

"And then I abandoned you. I still feel really bad about that."

"It doesn't matter now."

"I think we should talk about what happened to you," he said.

Brittany shook her head. "This has been a nice day. Why ruin it? I really don't want to talk about that."

"Why? You gave a fireside about it, didn't you?"

"Oh, you want me to give you my standard fireside talk, is that it?" she asked.

"Yes, that's what I want."

"I will, but only if you can quote the Young Women's theme."

" . . . strive to live the young women values which are . . . blah, blah, blah," he said in a falsetto voice.

She pointed an accusing finger at him and pushed him away. "It's very clear to me, sir, that you are an impostor."

"I'm serious, Brittany."

In her mind she tried out all the ways she could start. "I don't think I can talk to you about it," she finally said.

"Why not?"

"Because you're just back from a mission, which means you're too noble and good. Maybe you'll tell me it doesn't matter to you, and maybe it won't at first. But after a while, your imagination will start in. You'll picture what it was like, then you'll decide you can't handle the truth, so you'll quit being my friend. I'd rather leave it this way. You can walk away right now and that'll be okay with me because, after all, we're just friends. But we've had a nice time today. Let's not ruin it. Let's just walk away from this before we both get hurt."

"We can't ignore it."

"Why not?" she asked.

"Because I want to keep seeing you."

She shook her head. "Oh, c'mon, Craig, there are plenty of girls down in Utah. Get acquainted with them. If you won't do it for me, do it for fuel conservation."

"Why didn't you come to my homecoming?" he asked.

"Because you remind me of the play, and that reminds me of Derek, and that reminds me of things I don't want to remember."

"Are you saying there's no hope for us?" he asked.

"That's right. I don't think there is, Craig."

"Maybe you should get some counseling to help you deal with this," he said.

She threw up her hands. "You think you have the answer to everything, don't you? Well, you don't, okay? I've had hours and hours of counseling, both from my bishop and from a professional. What do you think counseling does, make it so it didn't happen? Well, that's not what it does."

"What has counseling done for you, if you won't talk about what happened to you?"

She glared at him. "Who do you think you are to ask me something like that?"

"Why are you so mad at me?" he complained.

"Why? Because you bring back all those memories from high school. On campus at Ricks I can go days without thinking about Derek. But seeing you brings it all back to me. I don't like that. I don't like that at all." She shook her head. "Why did you come up here to see me anyway?"

"I'll tell you some other time."

"Why some other time?" she asked.

"Because it's not the right time to tell you."

"When will be the right time?"

211

"I don't know. We'll both know when it's the right time."

"Oh, c'mon, Craig, you're not going to make the number one mistake of returned missionaries, are you?"

"What mistake?"

"You get off your mission realizing the next big step in life is marriage. So you pray about it and get some vague impression that you're supposed to marry some girl you used to know."

Craig was blushing enough that she knew she'd nailed it. "If that's what this is all about, you can forget it because I'm not going to do something just because you feel like it's the next thing to do."

"Like I said, this is not the right time to talk about this," Craig said.

She didn't know why she was feeling so angry. But she glared at him. "The right time? Look, as far as I'm concerned, it will never be the right time. Excuse me, I can't let you slow me down any longer. I need to get off this mountain." She took off running down the trail.

It felt good to run. She needed to get away from Craig and all he reminded her of. She didn't want to depend on anyone ever again. She wanted to be independent and free.

At first the trail was good for running—fairly smooth and straight, but within a few minutes, it became strewn with rocks sticking out of the ground. She had worn a pair of light tennis shoes, and it was a challenge to pick a good place to put her feet as she ran.

In one especially rough place, with all her weight on one foot, her ankle rolled, resulting in a severe sprain. She took just two more painful steps and hopped to a stop.

She didn't want Craig to find her that way, so she tried to continue, but each step was very painful. Finding a walking stick, she hobbled along as best she could.

Craig soon caught up with her. "Are you okay?" he asked.

212

"I just turned my ankle, that's all. I'm okay, really. You go on without me. I'll catch up with you. It's starting to feel better already."

She took a step. Her ankle hurt even more than before. She grimaced. "Really, I'm fine, just go on."

"I'm not leaving you. Don't be so stubborn, Brittany. Let me help you."

"I don't need your help."

He came to her side. "Put your arm around my waist."

"Why can't you understand that I don't want your help?"

She gritted her teeth and took two steps by herself. She paid for it though, because her ankle was throbbing with pain.

"Brittany?" he said.

She turned around. "What!"

"You've got to let me help you. We need to get down to the dock by six if we're going to catch the last boat. If we don't, we'll have another three miles to hike."

"Don't you think I know that?" She tried a few more steps, but it hurt too much. "I just need to rest for a minute, that's all." She sat down and took off her one shoe and touched her ankle to see how bad it was. It was already swollen and starting to discolor. She could tell it was hopeless. "I guess I might need some help."

"Okay."

He helped her get to a standing position. She put her right arm around his waist and took a step. It hurt, but not as bad.

"That's better," she said.

It was slow going. Hikers now were passing them regularly. Everyone wanted to get to the dock before the last boat left. Some offered to help but there wasn't much anyone could do.

The trail from Inspiration Point down to Hidden Falls

was the worst because it was steep and had been cut out of the side of a cliff. It was all rocks.

"It might be faster if you let me carry you," he said.

"What time is it?"

"Five-thirty."

She didn't want to miss the boat. "All right."

He carried her piggyback, carefully picking his way among the boulders on the trail.

By the time they reached Hidden Falls, the trail was deserted. Everyone had gone ahead of them.

"What time is it now?" she asked.

"Six-fifteen."

"We missed the boat," she said.

"Looks that way."

"I'm sorry."

"It doesn't matter. The trail around the lake is pretty flat."

Since they'd missed the boat, they were in no hurry, and they stopped occasionally to rest and share a bottle of water and a bag of trail mix from Brittany's day pack.

He'd backed up to a boulder to give her a place to sit, and he was leaning against the rock next to her, catching his breath.

"I bet you wish I'd gone on that diet now, right?" she teased.

"Not at all. You're fine, really."

"You make a pretty good packhorse."

Craig pretended to get emotional. Wiping an imaginary tear from his cheek, he said, "Thank you. That's one of the nicest things you've ever said to me."

Brittany couldn't help smiling. "Why did you even come to see me this weekend? You shouldn't be wasting your time with me. There are plenty of girls in Utah."

"I want to be with *this* girl."

"You're making a big mistake."

"I don't think so."

She leaned forward and rested her head on his back. They were quiet for a moment.

"How's the ankle?"

"Throbbing."

They fell silent for a few moments, then Craig said, "Derek hurt you real bad, didn't he?"

Brittany didn't immediately reply. Finally, she said, "Yes, he did."

"It must have been terrifying for you."

They avoided eye contact. After a moment Brittany said, "I tried to make him stop, but he was too strong. It was so awful. I didn't know someone I thought was my friend could be so cruel. Even now, whenever I think I've put it behind me, it keeps coming back."

She turned her head away, "Craig, I'm not sure I can be a wife. I'm not sure I can do what wives do."

"That wouldn't matter. I'd still want to marry you." He reached for her hand.

"How can you say that? Of course it matters."

"Whatever it takes, we'll work through it," he said. "I can wait for you until you're ready, even after we're married, if that's what you need."

"No, that wouldn't be fair to you."

"Whatever you need, that's what we'll do."

"Why?"

He lifted her face so he could look into her eyes. "Because I love you."

Brittany turned her head away. "When did you decide that?"

"Toward the end of my mission. I hadn't even been thinking about you, but one night I had a dream about you."

"What kind of a dream?"

He smiled to himself and shook his head slowly. "The most wonderful dream in the world."

"Are you going to tell me about it?" she asked.

"Not now. Later maybe."

"Why not tell me now?" she asked.

"It wouldn't be of much help to you. I can wait for you to catch up with me."

"The way I'll be hobbling around for a while there's not much likelihood of that," she said, smiling and trying to lighten the mood.

Craig didn't want to kid around. "Look, I'll be up here next weekend, and the weekend after that, and the weekend after that. For as long as it takes. We need time to get reacquainted."

"Are you sure about this?"

"I'm sure."

"If you get back home, meet a girl, and change your mind, I'll understand."

"That's not going to happen, Brittany."

"We'll see."

"You don't believe me, do you?"

"You just got off a mission, Craig. You've spent two years trying to help people. Your interest in me might be because you want to help me. But that's really not a very good reason to marry somebody. I just want you to consider other possibilities. That's all I'm saying. Wanting to rescue someone is not a good reason to get married."

"That's not what this is about. This goes way back to *My Fair Lady*."

"Well, we'll see how it goes. All I'm saying is, I'll understand if you change your mind."

"Would you stop with this? I love you, and that's not going to change."

"All right."

He stood up and flexed his back. "We'd better get started again."

He carried her piggyback along the path that ran beside the lake.

"I feel really safe with you," she said.

"Great," he said with a smile. "I'll try not to fall into the lake then."

"You want me to sing for you?" she asked.

"Absolutely."

She sang, "I Could Have Danced All Night" from *My Fair Lady*.

They made it to the car about nine that night. It was slower going in the dark and by then, Craig was tired.

They drove to Jackson Hole and went through the drive-through at a taco place before heading back to Rexburg. Brittany fell asleep in the car. She didn't wake up until they were just outside of town.

"How you doing?" Craig asked.

"I can't believe I slept so long," she said.

"I'm glad you did."

"Why? Were you getting tired of talking to me?"

"No. It means you feel safe with me."

"I do."

"I'm glad. What time is church tomorrow?"

"Nine."

"I'll pick you up about ten minutes to nine then."

"Are you going to carry me into church too?" she asked.

"If you want me to."

She smiled. "All the other girls will throw themselves down the stairs so you'll have to carry them around too."

"They'll have to get someone else. I'm reserved."

When they arrived at the place where she lived, Craig carried her up the stairs into her apartment.

"Where do you want me to drop you off? On your bed?"

She was surprised she didn't panic as he carried her into her room and gently set her down on her bed.

"I'll be going now."

"Thanks, Craig. That was quite an effort."

"No problem. See you in the morning." With that, he left.

She needed to talk to someone, so, while soaking her ankle in ice water, she telephoned her mother. They talked for over an hour. Brittany had some questions that she could only ask her mother, questions about the intimacies in marriage.

"The love that a husband and wife share is about giving," her mother said. "What Derek did to you was *take*. In marriage it will be totally different. I don't think you have anything to worry about. If you do end up marrying Craig, I'm sure he will be very sensitive to your wishes. The love shared by the two of you will make everything else seem natural and good. Do you trust Craig?"

"Yes."

"If you can trust him now, you'll be able to trust him when you're married. If he's as sensitive as you say, I'm sure he would never do anything that would make you feel uncomfortable."

Brittany felt better.

"Do you love him?" her mother asked.

"I *like* him. But I'm not sure I *love* him. He says he had a dream about me while he was on his mission. He wouldn't tell me what is was about, but it apparently made him think we should get married. At first it made me mad when he told me that."

"Why did it make you mad?" her mother asked.

"I don't like some guy telling me what I need to do."

"You're right about that."

"That's why he didn't want to tell me. He says he wants it to happen naturally, that we should fall in love, and not try to force anything."

"That sounds like a good idea," her mother said.

"I'm scared about the idea of getting married. That seems like a very adult thing to do. I don't feel old enough to be married."

"If you spend time together, maybe you'll find that you

can't stand to be apart. If that happens, then it's time to get married."

Brittany felt better after talking to her mother. She got ready for bed, then said her prayers. She had a lot to say to Father in Heaven.

She was very tired, but before she climbed into bed, she sat at her desk and looked at a pedigree sheet from a family history class she was taking. She read the names of the women, all relatives of hers, who had forged the chain of life from generation to generation. She wondered about each one and wished she could talk to them and find out what they were like when they were her age. They were a part of her, and their lives, the good and the bad, were a part of her heritage.

Life goes on, she thought.

15

It was probably good that Craig showed up only for weekends because it gave Brittany time to think. Sometimes she resented Craig's effort to win her heart.

Mindy, who was waiting for Rhett while he served a mission, was not much help. The first time she saw a picture of Craig, she said, "My gosh, Brittany, he looks so spiritual!"

"What happened to *hot?*" Brittany asked. "Last summer every guy you saw was *hot.*"

"Well, I was young and immature then," she kidded. "Now I can see that there are more important things."

"That's just because Rhett is on a mission."

Mindy shook her head. "It has nothing to do with that."

"I don't want to get married now, but that's all Craig can think about," Brittany said.

"How do you know?"

"Because he never talks about it."

Mindy burst out laughing. "Well, sure, that makes perfect sense!"

"Craig knows if he talks about us getting married, I'll panic and maybe even break up with him."

"So, what do you want to do?" Mindy asked.

"I want to date freshmen boys the rest of my life. I want to be the one who sends them on their missions."

"Not me," Mindy said. "I'm ready to move to the next level."

Knowing that, Brittany felt as though she'd lost an ally in Mindy. *How can I trust someone who's in sympathy with the enemy?* she thought.

The next Thursday, when Craig called to firm up their plans for the weekend, Brittany was in a bad mood. "I don't see why you're coming up again. I mean, what do we have in common, besides the fact we were in *My Fair Lady* together?"

"We liked each other then, didn't we?"

She almost hated to admit it. "Well, yeah, I guess so."

"Then let's just see what happens now, okay? From now on, we won't worry about the future. We'll just have fun. How does that sound?"

It was hard to argue against having fun. "Okay, but look, there's something you need to know about me."

"What?"

"I've taken *Missionary Preparation.*"

"So?"

"I am quite familiar with the commitment pattern."

"I don't get it."

"Don't try using it on me, okay?"

"Why would I do that? You've already been baptized."

Brittany felt foolish for even bringing it up.

The next day Craig showed up in one of her classes just before it began. "Excuse me, is this seat taken?" he asked.

"Yes, it is. Sorry," she said, trying to hide her delight in seeing him again.

"What about this other seat?" he asked, pointing to another vacant desk next to her.

"That's taken too."

"Are all these seats taken?" he asked.

"Yes, afraid so." She tried to look like she was much too busy studying to give him any time.

"Amazing. Well, if you don't mind, I'll just sit here until the regular occupant comes."

"I'm studying for a quiz. Would you mind keeping the noise down?"

"Oh, sure, no problem," he whispered. He kept quiet for all of thirty seconds. "You know, I've heard a lot about this class. I mean it's, like, world famous."

"Really?" she said, not even bothering to look up.

"Oh, yes."

"If you know so much, I'm sure you can tell me the name of the course, can't you?"

"Sure." His eyes darted to the cover of her textbook, which she quickly covered with a notebook.

"I'm waiting."

"It's . . . Prehistoric Recipes 101."

She smiled. "Really?"

"Oh, yes. It's a pretty easy class actually."

"Why's that?"

"Because every recipe starts out with, *Kill a woolly mammoth.*"

She made a strange gurgling sound while trying not to laugh.

Speaking in a scholarly tone, Craig said, "Oh, I see they've taught you the mating call of the woolly mammoth."

Brittany couldn't help it. She broke up laughing and was still giggling when the teacher entered the classroom. "What's so funny, Brittany?" he asked.

"Nothing."

"Do you have a guest with you today?"

"Yes, this is my friend Craig Weston. He just got off a mission."

"Craig, welcome to class," the teacher said.

"Thank you." Craig stood up and said to the instructor,

"When Brittany was in high school, she used to sell flowers on street corners. Her language was pretty rough. She swore a lot in those days, but I tutored her to the point where she learned to speak properly."

"Really?" the teacher said, not knowing whether to believe Craig or not.

Brittany just shook her head.

Craig continued. "Actually, I'm pretty sure my tutoring is responsible for her getting into Ricks. Let me ask a question, though, just to check up on her. Has she sworn much in this class?"

The teacher thought about it. "Well, not so far, but of course I haven't handed back her last exam yet. We might hear from her then."

Brittany needed to defend herself. "Craig and I were in a play together in high school," Brittany said. "That's what he's babbling about."

"What play?"

"*My Fair Lady.*"

"Oh, I get it," the teacher said. "Well, you're welcome to stay, Mr. Higgins. That is, if Miss Doolittle will behave herself."

After class, Craig gave Brittany a ride to her apartment. "If you could do anything tonight, what would it be?"

Brittany scowled. "This is Rexburg, Craig. There's not that much to do. We can either go to a movie or to a dance."

"I'm sure there's more to do than that. You just need to be a little more creative, that's all."

"Be my guest, Craig."

They ended up going to a movie.

On the next day, a Saturday, they went swimming at a natural hot springs swimming pool at Green Canyon. As Brittany was changing, she thought about getting into the pool. She was uneasy about having Craig see her in a

223

swimming suit. Not that the suit was revealing. It was a gray, one-piece suit she'd had for years.

By the time she padded in bare feet into the swimming area, Craig was already in the water. He climbed up the pool steps, offered his hand, and escorted her into the water.

"It's nice," she said as they stood together in waist-deep water. Apparently he also was a little self-conscious. "I gained a little weight on my mission," he said.

"Really? I didn't notice. You look fine."

"Thanks. You look good too," he said. But then he grimaced. "I'm sorry. I shouldn't have said that, should I?"

"No, it's okay, really."

"If I ever say anything wrong, just tell me, okay?" he said.

"I will, but don't worry about it."

It was a Saturday afternoon and the pool was filled with families and younger children. It wasn't really a place for swimming laps. Too many people for that. But there was a basketball hoop. Craig and Brittany rented a ball and practiced shooting. After a while, they moved to the diving board. They both only knew one basic dive, but they took turns practicing for a while.

After they tired of diving, they ended up standing in chest-deep water, watching the families with young children playing together.

A mother who looked to be about her age caught Brittany's eye. She had a two-year-old boy. Her husband, tall, still in his twenties, was taking great delight in introducing his son to the adventures of swimming. He supported the child with one hand under his stomach, the other on his back, walking him through the water. "You're swimming, Tyler! Do you like it?" he asked. From the smile on the boy's face, it was obvious he did like it.

Brittany couldn't take her eyes off them. The young father was tan only on his arms and neck; the rest of his body was white. He wore a beard, but it was neatly trimmed.

His wife had dark brown, short hair; high cheekbones; and a remarkably pretty face. She was a natural beauty.

The two young parents didn't seem to be aware of anyone else in the pool. They were there for their son, and he had their total attention.

Brittany would have liked to talk to the young mother and ask her a hundred questions about her life with her husband and young son. She could see how wrapped up they were in their little boy, how his every smile and whimper were important to them. She tried to imagine what their life together was like. Did they live in an apartment or a house? How long had they been married? What was it like for the woman to have a baby of her own? She wondered if they were members of the Church, and if they'd been married in the temple. She hoped they had.

Their little boy was adorable. Brittany tried to imagine herself being a young mother. *That could be Craig and me someday.* The thought just came.

Craig caught her studying the young parents. "They look happy, don't they?" he said.

"Yeah, they do."

A few minutes later they decided to try another pool. The water in it was too warm to do anything but sit in the water and talk. By now, Brittany was beyond feeling self-conscious about being in her swimming suit around Craig. *Like it or not, Craig, this is the way I am.* They were down to the basics now; any makeup she might have worn into the pool had long since washed away. Her hair had been wet enough times that any styling she might have given it that day had been erased. It was the same for Craig. He'd long ago quit trying to arrange his hair so it wouldn't look like it was thinning. Actually, she liked it better that way.

The warmer water lulled her into a drowsy sense of well-being. If she had worries, she couldn't remember what they were.

"What did you learn on your mission?" she asked.

He got a thoughtful, faraway look in his eye. "I learned a lot of things. Where do you want me to begin?"

"What was the hardest lesson you learned on your mission?"

He seemed surprised by her question. He turned to see if her expression would give him a clue about what she was driving at.

"You're not the same now, are you?" she said.

"Why do you say that? What have you noticed that's different about me?"

"In high school you came across like you were a political ad for a presidential candidate. I mean, I could almost hear the narrator as the camera followed you around school." She spoke in an announcer's voice: "*Even as a youth, Craig Weston demonstrated the vision and clearthinking generally found only in older men. 'Born to lead' is how one classmate described him. The awards and honors continued to pile up—member of the student senate, senior class president, 3.94 grade point average, winner of the coveted Scholarship for Youth Excellence . . . blah, blah, blah.*"

Wearing an embarrassed grin, Craig splashed a little water on Brittany. "You sure know how to hurt a guy, don't you?"

"Not really. The thing is I don't see that in you anymore."

"You mean I'm no longer promising?" he teased.

"No, you're plenty promising. It's just that you seem less impressed with yourself than you used to be. What happened on your mission to change you?"

He nodded, acknowledging the question, but didn't answer right away. When he started to talk, his voice was soft. "Scotland is not a high-baptizing mission. In the beginning I was certain I was going to turn that around, that I would be a modern-day Ammon and end up baptizing thousands. I worked hard, and managed to get a few baptisms, but nowhere as many as I had planned.

"At first I thought it was all up to me. My companion and I used to set goals on how many baptisms we were going to have the next month. We'd set high goals, not based on the people we were teaching, but on how many we felt we should have. And then we convinced ourselves that our goal was what Father in Heaven had in store for us if we'd work hard. At the end of every month, when we'd fall far below our goal, we'd tell ourselves that it was because we had done something wrong, and that it was all our fault because we weren't faithful or not working hard enough or whatever. That was not a happy time for me. I felt like a failure.

"It was a new experience for me. It was the first time I'd run into something I couldn't excel at. That was hard for me to take."

"Did you go your whole mission feeling that way?" she asked.

He shook his head. "No. Our mission president heard about the way we were setting goals and counseled us to stop. He told us a goal was not something you should use to beat yourself up. He told us to set more realistic goals. And then he told us to trust in the Savior, that He is our partner. He explained that nobody wants baptisms as much as the Lord does, but even He can't do anything if a person is not willing to listen. That changed me. My emphasis went from doing what would make me look good to trying to do what the Lord wanted me to do.

"Just that change in attitude made all the difference in the world for me. Once I learned that my mission wasn't about making myself look good, then things began to go much better for me. I learned to forget myself and just love the people I was working with. That's what's important—to love the people . . . no, it's more than that . . . it's to love the people with the same kind of love the Savior has for them. He does

227

love them, you know. Every one of them. Once I learned that, then I felt peace in my heart."

She nodded. "That's what I see when I look in your eyes then, isn't it?"

"You can see that in my eyes?"

"I think so." His right hand was underwater. She reached for it.

"Is that you?" he asked.

"Yeah, why?"

"At first I was afraid it was a dead fish."

"A *dead fish!* Thanks a lot, Craig." She jerked her hand away and sent a spray of water into his face.

"Actually, you can't do that," he said calmly.

"Really? Well, I just did. And, look. I can do it again." She splashed him again.

"Notice that I'm exercising total restraint," he said, wearing just a hint of a smile on his dripping face.

She snickered. "Yes, I noticed that. That's great. Let's see some more of it," she teased, splashing him again.

"Do you want me to come after you? Is that what you wish?" he asked politely. She wondered if the reason he was asking was because of Derek.

"You don't scare me, Craig. Not at all." This time she stood up and used both hands to scoop a mountain of water into his face.

"Don't press it, Brittany. I have my limits."

She spotted a small bucket. Climbing out of the pool, she retrieved the bucket, jumped back in, filled the bucket, and slowly poured the water over his head.

"All right, that's it!" He lunged for her but missed.

She turned to run away from him, but trying to run in the water was like performing a ballet in slow motion. He caught up with her, and she turned to splash him. Before she could do it again, he grabbed her hand. She felt a little shiver of panic when he first grabbed her, and noticing her reaction, he quickly released his grip.

The water fight continued. Both of them were laughing and shouting warnings at each other. At one point in their water battle, he turned his back to her and she used the opening to grab him from behind and wrap her arms around his chest. "I've got you now, Craig. You might as well give up."

"Not a chance," he shot back. He flailed his arms wildly and whirled in a circle, but it was all show. She lifted up her legs and let him turn her in a circle, for just a moment resting her head on his back. She was surprised how much she enjoyed the feeling of being physically close to him.

She continued to hold on tightly, even when he stooped down, submerging them both, then leaped up out of the water. He did it several times while Brittany held on and laughed at his puny efforts to shake her off his back.

Winded, he finally stopped struggling. "I give up," he said. "You win."

She released her grip and stepped away from him, and they stood there, looking at each other and grinning.

"That was so much fun!" she said.

He was breathing hard. He shook his head. "That's your idea of fun? Beating up on an out-of-shape returned missionary?" he said, sitting down on the pool steps. Brittany waded over and sat next to him, reaching to hold his hand under water. They sat like that until he caught his breath.

Finally, he said, "I've told you what I learned on my mission. What did you learn about life while I was gone?"

She thought back over the past three years. She never would have asked for what had happened to her, but, even so, she had learned some valuable lessons. *But where do I begin.*

After thinking about it, she said, "I guess I'd say two things. First of all, that I didn't need to feel guilty or repent because of what happened to me. The other thing is, that through the Atonement of Jesus Christ, sorrow can be removed." As she said it, she realized that she wasn't entirely there yet, but it was coming. She even felt that someday she might be able to forgive Derek for what he had done to her.

Craig was looking into her eyes, listening to her answer. A little smile on her face, she softly said, "I've learned . . . that Jesus Christ is the only one who can make things that are wrong turn out right. No matter how awful something is, He can remove the pain."

Craig squeezed her hand. "Isn't it strange that we should both learn the same thing—me in Scotland and you in Utah and Idaho?"

She didn't answer right away. "Maybe that's the only lesson worth learning."

"It is," he said in a husky voice.

She looked over at him. They were a pair, all right—waterlogged enough for their fingers to be puckered, his body an unnatural white from being on a mission in Scotland for two years, where, when the sun shone, people wondered what the strange object was in the sky, or so he'd told her.

She was in no better shape. The suit she was wearing was a dull gray, not flashy like some of the girls in the pool, but it was what she felt comfortable in, both for modesty, and for allowing her to melt into the background, which was where she wanted to be for any stranger who might be watching her in the swimming pool.

Craig no longer needed to play *student leader,* and she no longer needed the applause of the crowd. She still enjoyed singing, and she did perform in public, but, somehow, it wasn't as important to her as it had once been.

What she considered important in her life had changed. What she cared most about now was the Savior, Father in Heaven, and her mom. There was also her family that stretched back in time. She knew many of her ancestors by name; she had been baptized for some of them, and someday, when the time was right, she'd be endowed in behalf of those women.

They decided to leave the pool. Barefoot, they walked gingerly back to the dressing area and separated.

On the drive home, Brittany asked if she could sit on the divider between the seats, at least until they reached the highway. Craig told her it would be bumpy riding there, but she said she didn't mind as long as she could be closer to him. She made the move.

As they started down the dusty dirt road, she rested her head on his shoulder and ran her fingertips lightly back and forth across his right arm.

He invited her to come down to Utah the next weekend for a big family reunion. It would give her a chance to get to know his grandparents and aunts and uncles. "They all want to meet you," he said.

"Sure, I'd like to meet them too," she said. *I should be worried about meeting his entire family, but I'm not,* she thought. *Maybe I will marry Craig someday, but I'm not going to tell him right away. I want to enjoy this part of our life together. We still need to become better friends, and then fall more in love, and then I'll tell him my decision.* She smiled. *Or maybe I'll just wait for him to use the commitment pattern on me.*

She touched his lips with her finger, and he looked over at her and smiled.

I've come a long way, she thought. *Considering the uphill battle I've had to face, I've done about as well as anyone could have. I still have my faith in Heavenly Father. I still have my testimony. And I have a wonderful guy at my side. I know that love in marriage is good. I love the temple. I'm going to be endowed as soon as I can, and then go back again and again. Craig and I will have children. We'll love them with all our hearts, and we'll teach them the right way to live. In spite of all I've been through, all the dreams I've ever had are still possible. What more could I ask for?*

She could see a mountain jutting up in front of them. Looking at it, she remembered how Julia always talked about getting to the other side of the mountain.

The other side of the mountain, she thought. *Actually, I think I'm already there.*

TEN IDEAS TO HELP YOU STAY SAFE

1. Follow the guidelines in *For the Strength of Youth*: "When you begin dating, go in groups or on double dates. Avoid pairing off exclusively with one partner. Make sure your parents meet and become acquainted with those you date. . . . You may occasionally want to invite your dates to activities with your family.

   Plan positive and constructive activities when you are together. Do things that help you get to know each other. Be careful to go to places where there is a good environment."

2. Always live the Word of Wisdom and date only boys who do the same.

3. Trust your parents' feelings. If they have uneasy feelings about a boy, talk to them and find out why they feel that way. One good way to determine a boy's intentions is to invite him to a family activity.

4. Find out the reputation of a boy you are about to see. If people say he has a bad temper, drinks alcohol, or is known to treat girls as inferiors, stay away from him.

5. Learn how to say no when you don't want to go out with a boy. Don't give the excuse, "I'm busy this weekend," because he may keep asking until you run out of excuses. Make it clear from the beginning that you don't want to go out with him—not now and not ever. "I just don't want to go out with you, that's all." (There's no law that says you have to be nice all the time.)

6. When a boy comes to pick you up for the first time, let your parents grill him for a few minutes before you show up to rescue him. Let your dad (or mom or older brother or home teacher) ask him all those really embarrassing questions—about his educational and career plans, his

family, his testimony, when he will be bringing you home, and what he has planned for your date. Later, you can apologize to him for how pushy your parents are, but let them do what parents do so well—demonstrate their protective attitude toward their daughter.

7. When you're with a boy, be clear in your communications. Say what you mean. Don't be passive. Have definite opinions about where to go and what to do. Practice saying no, without smiling, so there can be no doubt that you mean no. If you need to, get a choir leader or drama teacher to show you how to project your voice.

8. Until you are married, never be in a bedroom alone with a man or boy, no matter how well you know him or how innocent-sounding the reason he gives to invite you there.

9. Making out is not an innocent pastime. Don't send signals that can be misinterpreted. If you don't understand this, ask a parent or trusted adviser.

10. Trust your "gut-level" feelings. If you ever feel unsafe in any situation, *get out,* even if it means you have to make a *big scene.* In fact, once in a while, with your parents' coaching, practice making big scenes.